THE DATING GAME

MODERN ROMANCE SHORT STORIES

LEIGH ALDER   STELLA ALMAZAN   SKYE BALLANTYNE

NATALIE CARROLL   SHARI HELD   DAVID LANGE

MATT J. MCGEE   ARIK MITRA   TIM O'NEAL   JOSH POOLE

LUISA KAY REYES   TRAVIS WELLMAN

The Dating Game–Modern Romance Short Stories

Copyright © 2023 by JK Larkin

Published by Red Penguin Books

Bellerose Village, New York

CONTENTS

GOOD TO SEE A SMILE
TRAVIS WELLMAN AND JOSH POOLE

"Mask, wallet, keys, phone," Caroline said to herself as she checked the items in her purse.

"You've been saying that over and over all day. Just go get in your truck and drive to the restaurant," Madison groaned from the kitchen.

"I still have half an hour until my date, and I'll spend it however I please," Caroline retorted as she dropped her purse down on the couch.

"Look, I get that this is your first date since the pandemic started, but you're blowing things out of proportions. It's not like it's that big of a deal. You're both fully vaccinated now, and you got your booster," Madison said, walking into the living room with a pack of cookies in one hand and a glass of milk in the other.

"It's also my first date since I recovered from Covid, and I know this should be perfectly safe, but the anxious part of my brain just won't shut off. What if I get sick again? What if this time it's worse? What if his profile and the little 'VACCINATED' sticker he has is all bullshit?" Caroline's heart sped up as her mind flashed back to laying in bed, a shivering, feverish mess struggling to breathe between spasms of coughing. Meanwhile, Madison had become one with her recliner and dunked a cookie into a cool glass of milk.

"I get that. I got sick too if you'd remember, but we both got better and now, since we're both still alive, I think it's time we both get back in the saddle," Madison replied before extracting the cookie from the glass of milk and biting into the soft morsel.

"If it's time for both of us to get back in the saddle, why aren't you going on a date?"

Madison looked contemplative as she crunched through a cookie. "I'm not going on a date, because the only attractive guy in this podunk town asked you out already. I tried all the apps, there's like seven people here and they're all from the wrong century."

"You don't even like men!"

"You're right... Let me rephrase that. If there were any ravishing and available lesbians around here I would also be going out tonight. Instead, I have a date with these cookies and maybe a nice hot bath afterward," Madison replied.

"Alright, fair enough." Caroline looked through the contents of her purse again.

"You're going to keep doing that until you're late." Madison flicked her hand and inadvertently flung milk everywhere.

"No, because it's a five-minute drive into town and I don't have to be there for half an hour. You want me to crunch the numbers?"

Madison didn't reply, opting instead to stuff another soggy cookie into her mouth and roll her eyes. Caroline checked her purse one last time before rushing off to the bathroom to triple-check her makeup and hair. Everything was arranged properly, and in its place. Every shade, every tone, and every strand of hair was immaculate. All that was left was to take a breath, and remember to drive with the windows up so all her hard work didn't blow out into a tangled, chaotic mess. She walked back through the living room and towards the front door, devoted entirely to the mission at hand. Madison did nothing but wave goodbye and give a soft, optimistic laugh as the slamming door declared that the game was on.

In spite of being ten minutes early for her date, she could see her date's Jeep already sitting in the sparsely-populated restaurant parking lot. One of the few perks of living in a town with a population of only a thousand was that you could identify just about anyone by their vehicles alone even if you'd never met them and even if you'd only been there for just over a year. It made using dating apps all the stranger, as you would garner details about people you recognized but didn't know. She strained her eyes to see if he was inside his Jeep as she drove by, but the tint on his windows made it hard to tell.

She pulled her truck into a spot a few spaces down from his car, and sat in the driver's seat to think of what greeting she should use as the sun set over the nearby mountains. Rehearsing her lines, she stared at her confident face in the tiny mirror that deployed from the sun visor and wondered if she'd do everything wrong the moment the spotlight was on her. She opened the app again, looking through his profile and trying to find any last-minute excuses to bail. The thought shook her, but with the practiced motion of over a year's worth of experience she reached into her purse and affixed her mask to her face.

———

Visualize an orchard, the flowers, the pollen sweeping through the air over the soft grass. Collect your thoughts under the tree, let your eyes wander. Say whatever falls into your head, and hope she doesn't think you're an idiot.

"What's the difference between a malbec and a merlot?" He asked, poised at the table like Rodin's *Thinker* as he perused the predominantly French menu for any semblance to words he knew.

"Malbec belongs in the smoker's section," she replied in a rainy, nervous voice. "Are you a smoker?"

"No," he replied, pointing at the dimple on his chin. "I dated a smoker once. Whenever we kissed my chin would put out the cigarette."

"You know" she began, "I never know if anything you say is true."

"Any idea how we ever got a decent French restaurant in this tiny town?"

"Stranger things have happened. Now streaming on Netflix," she said in an announcer's voice.

Her lips resolved to him for the first time since they'd been seated by the waiter, a man who had a conscious symmetry to his appearance, with a tie perfectly positioned, sleeves rolled up in exacting measures, and a centralized parting to his hair executed with Vermeer precision. Her lips were bright red, but against her sepia skin seemed natural, a piece of her own pallet that coexisted formally with the ochre of her fingernails and the explosive hues of her empire dress, a Jacobean Floral sea of copper, beige, and gold floating in maroon like mechanical suns. Her hair was a basket woven with Havana twists while a single braid strayed from the nexus and ran the scenic route down her cheek before falling ineffectually on her collar.

"Doodle me like one of your French girls," her eyes did a loop.

The waiter approached with a militant stride that, he sensed, concealed a sagging weariness from a long day of brief ordeals.

"We're going with the Merlot," his date declared before the waiter could, in his own perspicacious way, tell them what to get under the guise of asking very specific questions. An art that took little insight to detect, but a lifetime to perform.

"What's that like?" He asked

"Ah, the Chilean Merlot. I would say bold, smooth—"

"Like me," he leaned and whispered to his date.

"Soft, acidic, bit of a plum," the waiter finished, and his date grew the smile of someone who'd won an exchange without speaking.

"Sounds perfect," she replied, plucking the menu from his hand before reuniting it with her own and submitting them to the waiter like a test they'd confidently passed.

They sat quietly for some time, listening to the ambient noises of the busy restaurant and, he presumed on her behalf, the sound of their thoughts. The truth was, the date was the confluence of everything he'd ever wanted and everything he'd been warned about. An intelligent, seasoned, amicable person that wasn't from a thirty-mile radius of where he grew up. The truth was, that while he looked presentable wearing those khaki pants and gunmetal grey button-up for the first time since he'd bought it three years before, he scarcely kept himself from collapsing and pooling on the floor. He had the integrity of a waning crescent moon.

She probably knew Shakespeare and all sorts of writers he'd never heard of, and he didn't know anything but this: that a glass was for a rendezvous, but a bottle was a declaration. It was the only indication that things were going well aside from the smiles that he had difficulty interpreting, if they were genuine reflections of a romantic intrigue or just sparks of amusement. He wasn't sure if he should bring up what he did for a living, or how working as a housekeeper for all the local fraternity chapters was about as dignified and well-compensated as it sounded. He wanted to ask what it was like being an engineer who was also a woman without sounding horrible. Most of all, he wanted to be able to articulate anything without gridlocking his brain with the certainty that he was completely, imperially, ignorant.

"We'll be getting the steak right? That's what people do when they go to places like this? What's French for steak?" He spoke with a tone of mock-confusion to hide his actual confusion.

"I'm vegetarian, but you should indulge." She shrugged, seeming to have lost all interest in him to peruse the food menu.

The next great hurdle to bound over was the delicate task of ordering a steak properly done. He'd never met a vegetarian for all he knew. Did they feel similarly to the average middle-class omnivore? Should he order the steak medium-rare to put forth the notion that hhe ad a great deal of dignified air about him, but that he also wasn't a barbarian? Should he order it well-done to indicate that while, yes, he was an omnivore, that he believed in eating a product that was as far removed from the raw, natural, living state of the creature as possible?

"Were you always a vegetarian?" He asked, having found his own Ephialtes pass to betray any sincerity.

"No. A few years ago, I would've joined you with a steak," she replied, twirling her bronze bracelet around her narrow wrist.

"So, you would've just ordered it blue-rare and tenderized it with a club?"

"No, you have to do medium-rare at least to break down the collagen in the meat," she laughed, and the whiteness of her teeth made him lick the coffee-saturated stones of his own mouth insecurely.

"Sounds like you worked in a kitchen at some point?" He asked.

"All throughout college, yes. I worked in the dining hall and then worked in a fine dining place just off campus for post-grad."

He pursed his lips for a moment before following up, "did you like it?"

She gave a nod with her head that consisted of multiple, almost imperceptibly small motions, each rearranging the meaning of the previous one until what he was left with was a confused *I don't know, maybe some of it was okay.* He'd worked fast food before, and he imagined himself giving the same sort of nod if she had approached him with that very question.

"So, what are you looking for?" He asked, having never made the leap while they were messaging back and forth on an online dating app.

"Love and a dessert menu," she flipped the menu over, slapping the edge audibly against the white tablecloth with a dampened thud.

"It's in the middle, between the appetizers and the salads," he pointed it out.

"Oh, you're right," she paused for a moment. "That's a bit out of place for a dessert menu."

"What was that other thing you were looking for, again?"

"Love," she replied, with a blended look of anticipation and sarcasm.

"I can't help you with that one," he shrugged, and she let out a subdued laugh just as the waiter returned with the bottle of merlot.

He ordered a steak au poivre with a side of asparagus and small baked potatoes inundated in rosemary. She ordered cauliflower steak with a Romesco sauce and lentils, which he had never seen nor heard of before and assumed the worst. The waiter left as if he'd just remembered he left the oven on, which suited both of them just fine.

"So," she swirled the wine for a moment. "What do you do for a living, and what do you do for fun?"

He wasn't sure how to spin cleaning up after a frat to make it seem dignified or how to spin his hobby for collecting walnut husks that the squirrels left around the local park as an adrenaline-fueled, brave, ultra-masculine endeavor. In the end, he decided that honesty was, in spite of all of its faults, the proper way forward.

"I clean up frat houses for a living and for fun I pick up walnut shells that squirrels chew on. I don't do anything creative with the shells, I just keep them in boxes because I'm convinced that someday I'll think of something." He blurted out his response before shoving a smoldering potato into his mouth to chew rapidly as a way to bring closure to his rant.

"You know, that actually sounds really interesting. The walnut shells, not the frat thing." She replied, excising a tiny morsel of the cauliflower with a fork and knife.

"Really?"

"Yeah. My work has always taken up all of my time, and before when I was in college it was the same but with classes and shifts at the restaurant. Hobbies have always eluded me, so it's like this great forbidden, unexplored domain."

From there, the conversation changed, covering the households that they grew up in, how he'd spent most of his life living in a small trailer park just off of the interstate before moving into the small southern Virginia town where they were dining. How she'd grown up just outside of Baltimore in a little suburb that sounded like it could've been from any 80s slasher film, but had spent time all across Europe under the guise of an art major that allowed for much more opportunities abroad than engineering. He mentioned how he used to work on farms and shovel out horse stalls and she shared the stories of her time as an RA for her dorm hall at university. They discussed cult 70s indie horror and about how nothing made in the last ten years was worth its weight in pig's blood, and how she'd somehow found her way into the town, moving in with her friend on the outskirts and working remotely as a technical consultant on cell tower installs. The horror movie bit had of course played a huge role in their matching altogether. That and, as both of them had acknowledged, the abysmal dating pool in the area.

She looked over the dessert menu again, settling on a chocolate pudding cake and two small glasses of port. The cake came out adored with more ornamentation than a Roman victory parade, accompanied by two cheering glasses of vibrant, bright wine. Over cake and port, they talked again about what they were looking for, finding a confluence with only a few stones disrupting their currents. They talked about how using the app had made things awkward between them and people they knew, or at least thought they knew. How they'd seen almost all of their friends, coworkers, bosses, and even family members advertising some superficial trait or deep-end strangeness that never should have been broadcast to the world.

After the dinner, they walked outside before he walked her out to her car. He didn't see as she deleted the app that had brought them together. They thought quietly to themselves how it had been good, all of it. There was no shared thank you, no exchanging of numbers, only the silence as they exchanged a soft kiss and, wordlessly, they agreed to spend the night together at his embarrassing place downtown. With all the uncertainty there had been going into the date, and with all the uncertainty of things to come, both in the narrow sense of their potential future and in the larger scope of a world pandemic there was, at least, one simple truth. That it was good to see someone smile.

THE ACCIDENTAL POOLBOY

MATT MCGEE

The night before had been Paul's 42nd birthday. He'd waited all year but Shannon, his on and on and on girlfriend had merely helped a few friends recite the annoying annual song, then leaned over and pecked him on the cheek. There had been no after-party hotel room rattling with abandon, no make-out session in his car. Theirs wasn't a loveless relationship but, and his best friend Babe would agree, the days of red-hot loving had definitely cooled.

"And dude, Shannon's hot," Babe said. He'd dragged Paul out for post-party drinks. Empties stood around their corner booth table. "*Hot.*"

"Thanks. Yeah, she is. Just not for me anymore."

"OK. So do something unusual."

"Said the guy named after his grandfather's favorite baseball player."

"You gotta admit, it works."

"So if you're such a fan of relationships why don't you have a girlfriend?"

"When I've already got the whole world calling me Babe?"

. . .

In the morning Paul rubbed the night from his eyes. The thrumming in his head wasn't normal. It was worse than a hangover, dehydration or a queasy stomach. His gut was telling him something else:

Apathy. That's what it is. And it had taken hold - like rust, he thought.

Babe was right. Nothing new happened anymore. Ever. Drinking hadn't been different, though he'd hoped it would reveal some kind of magic. He always hoped for magic and was disappointed when it didn't show, but kept looking. Now his head throbbed as he recited the drunk's motto:

Never again.

The last thing he'd fallen into and really loved, besides Shannon, was acting; he'd been cast in a few plays and reveled in making his character as authentic as possible. But it'd been a while since he'd auditioned for anything, and besides, the one fan he wanted didn't approve of his passion.

Paul reached for the nightstand. Maybe turning on his phone would help. He tapped the power button.

A single voicemail. Shannon, no doubt. Afraid to be alone, she'd recite the details of her ride to work, the day ahead, someone who was driving her crazy with demands, and, finally, that she couldn't possibly get together tonight. She'd have something going on. Shannon always had something going on. It rarely included him.

He called his voicemail. A woman's voice came through.

"Hi Paul, this is Karen! Ninety-six Dune? Was just wondering if you'd be coming by to clean the pool today. OK. Thanks. Bye."

Click.

Paul was a metal fabricator. Mostly he made steel boxes. These boxes would be fitted with doors and made into cabinets, the majority of which would be shipped to fast food restaurants around the world and used as trash receptacles. He could go into a Jack in the Box, McDonald's or Wendy's almost anywhere in the world and see his life's work.

Paul's days consisted of sixteen points of spot welding, another box, another box, an occasional mistake that might be braised, recovered, otherwise it ended up in the scrap. Boxes and boxes and boxes. Occasionally Shannon. A text from Babe, taunting him to come out. He mostly ignored those, though he appreciated being remembered.

Paul had never cleaned a pool in his life. Well, he thought, that wasn't true. His Uncle Skeeter, some might have called him the family success, lived on a nicer side of town. Skeeter had a pool. He'd invited Paul for a swim one summer weekend; Paul reciprocated by taking out the skimmer and cleaning the surface of stray leaves. It wasn't exactly the beginning of a brilliant career.

Karen? Her voice sounded sweet. Mannered. Clear-spoken. Caucasian. In his imagination, she sounded pretty. He laid there, still in bed, and threw an arm behind his head.

Dune? Throughout his years in the city he'd delivered pizzas, auto parts, driven a cab, but he didn't remember any Dune Street. He opened Google Maps. The only 96 Dune Street was in another state.

He thought. Spelled with a UA? No, that would be Duane. A well-spoken, pretty Caucasian woman wouldn't pay a mortgage on a street named after the developer's mechanic.

Wait.

There'd been a snack company called Doone. He'd seen them in gas stations. Laura Doones? Sure. He Google-mapped 96 Doone.

Boom.

1.3 miles away. He tapped on the 'layer' feature. It showed every inch of Karen's asphalt driveway. Every neighbor's rooftop. And there it was.

A big, beautiful, aqua-green rectangle occupied a third of the yard. The rest was trees. Privacy was a concern for a hottie like Karen, no doubt. The trees looked like ash.

And those bastards probably shed year-round.

———

Paul called in sick at the box plant. He couldn't tell them he had a gig as a pool guy, though calling out on behalf of an acting job had its appeal. That's how he had to think of it. He stepped into the shower and took his time in the steaming water. Debbie, his landlady, wasn't home; no danger of her coming around, knocking on his door about running down the water heater and running up the water bill. He'd occasionally thought to let the shower run long and, when she came rapping, dare her to come in and turn it off herself. Debbie wasn't bad-looking and they'd flirted casually. But he had Shannon and no reason to rock the home lifeboat. No point thinking about it now anyway.

A pool needed cleaning.

His hand hit his dresser drawer. What do pool men wear? From his bottom drawer, he pulled a clean pair of Levi's, not his best but role appropriate. From the closet, a brown flannel. The shirt looked like something a guy of his new trade would wear this time of year. Might be a little cold. He looked back at the phone.

Still nothing from Shannon.

He fired up his third-hand Mazda. A neighbor a few doors away was doing some major excavation. *Maybe putting in a pool,* Paul thought. This could be the start of something. He could start a route. Buy some tools. He looked up their driveway; there was a dump truck, its white cab-forward, black bin tossed back in full tilt. A backhoe chugged black exhaust. Three men labored. The whole thing looked legitimate, the kind of project that had required a year's effort to get city permission.

Paul needed a truck. Babe would be no use there; he'd plunked everything he had into a Tesla. Nice, but not role-appropriate. *Better think of something or I'll lose Karen's job,* he thought.

Then Paul had an idea. He turned the car and sped a couple of blocks to the Carl's Jr. The smell of charbroiling hit his nose. At the intersection, standing on the corner was the reason he'd come.

The old man wore a Navy ball cap, green flak jacket and held a cardboard sign that described his hobo status. Paul swung into a parking place.

Twenty feet away the old man's wife sat in the passenger side of the couple's pride and joy, a 1972 Chevy C10. Wide mirrors had once helped tow a trailer they'd long ago sold. A small American flag waved from the radio antenna. Gray primer had mostly taken over where Army mint once shone. There is a step bumper. Perfect.

"How's business?"

The old man turned around.

"Well, hey!"

They'd seen each other around. Paul had limited his generosity to the form of non-judgmental friendship. In lieu of a handshake, the old man nodded his way.

"What's doin?"

"You want the long story or the short one?"

The old man turned back to traffic. Cars coming. He held up the sign.

"Let's go with short."

"Need a truck for a job I got lined up. Thought maybe you'd loan me the Chevy for an hour. Take my Mazda."

"What kinda job?"

"Pool cleaning."

The old man nodded. "Sounds easy enough. Need a hand?"

Sure, Paul thought, *and the old guy would enjoy himself. But the guy shouldn't be involved if it goes sideways.*

"One man job," Paul said reluctantly. "Probably only an hour. Just need a truck. Pool cleaning supplies, catcher, all that. Won't fit in the car," he nodded toward the Mazda.

The old man nodded, too. He drew an ancient key from his jacket pocket. Paul reached in his pants pocket and traded his Mazda key. The old lady would need a place to sit. They might have a recycling emergency. Either way, they'd have wheels.

"You know I've never asked," Paul decided to say, "how'd you two meet?"

"Just got back from 'Nam. I had a job at a bakery. She came past one day, saw me through the window. Started becoming a regular customer. Took me weeks to realize she'd become a regular customer just for me."

"We're so clueless," Paul admitted.

"We are. I got lucky. One day she called the bakery, said 'whoops, I dialed the wrong number!' but I took the opportunity to ask her out. Rest is history."

Paul just nodded. "She still got a sweet tooth?"

The old man held up his sign for a cluster or approaching cars. "Once a year I bake her a batch just like the ones I used to make."

"Keeping love alive. OK, well, I'll see you back here at," Paul pulled out his cell, "three. No later."

"Sounds good."

A young woman in a Honda tapped a honk. The old man leaned forward, accepted a bill.

"Thank you for your service!"

The old man gave a little salute. Paul descended the slope to the truck. The woman watched him approach. She looked up at the old man.

Paul looked back at the street corner. The old man nodded.

"She's part of the deal."

Paul shrugged. He'd always wanted an entourage.

———

The Chevy rode rough compared to his little import. The steering swayed like the pressure in all four tires were mismatched. Maybe it was. Maybe the old man couldn't stoop to attend to it anymore. Paul made a note to reset it for them. When he turned toward his house, the left wheel shouted out a heavy klunk. Nothing he could do about that without a lift. He turned into his neighborhood.

Up ahead stood a familiar white van, its wheels propped on a curb. The driver had plopped her over-full laundry basket on the lawn. She'd once been married to his Uncle Skeeter; the van was a divorce present intended to continue her dog grooming business. Paul knows she lives in the van, and last he heard she had one client left, a retired sports figure who kept her in gas money.

The old lady gave the slightest wave at his former aunt. The fallen aunt waved back.

Three blocks later Paul pulled affront his house and threw the truck in gear.

"Be right back."

The old woman nodded.

Paul lifted the latch on the side gate and kicked through the weeds that had overtaken the yard; he made a note to trim them for the landlady. Their pool was contained by a short blue-mesh safety fence. The blue tarp covering the surface was anchored by large rocks, bowed with a foot of rainwater and black sludge.

He found the skimmer every pool owner has. There was a sorry old orange-handled broom, its bristles bent, twisted, ruined by weather. He snatched it up too, along with a five-gallon bucket of 3" Jumbo Tabs, labeled 'stabilized chlorinating tablets for swimming pools.'

He'd learned the value of props.

When Paul had been cast in an Arthur Miller play, he learned that a man with a rifle over his shoulder is obviously a soldier, a guy in Levi's and a flannel with an axe over his shoulder is clearly a lumberjack, and today, as he marched thru the weeds and daffodils, a guy with a skimmer on a long pole and a bottle of chlorine tablets was Paul the Poolman.

Paul slipped into the laundry room thru a side door with a cracked window. He found a near-empty bottle of Clorox and poured its remnants into the kitchen sink. He flushed the sink with tap water then refilled the bottle. He screwed the cap back on, peeled away its label and smiled. He tossed everything into the truck bed.

He and the old lady passed the old man on their way to Doone. He stood in gray slacks and olive flak jacket, cardboard sign held at chest level. Someone rolled down a passenger window and made a donation; the old man gave the slightest tip of his hat. The old lady saw it but nothing registered on her face. Paul turned the truck north toward Doone. He breathed deeply, sharp, rapidly.

Time to get into character.

———

Karen's house is in a well-established, dutifully maintained neighborhood. Three generations have risen with the sun, stayed well-employed, rode out recessions and downturns without a blip in their bank accounts or even a browning of their manicured lawns. There are no night people on Doone Street unless they're renting a room from someone who's lonely, greedy, or both. His Uncle Skeeter lives nearby. Paul notes this, an emergency contact if needed.

Karen's house is a yellow one-story on a corner lot. A white mailbox stands sentry beside an unstained driveway and, beside that, a narrow strip of trim lawn. Come sundown a corner streetlamp will flicker to life and throw its pale, orange-yellow pall until morning. By then he'd be long gone.

Paul opened the truck's door with a squawk.

"I'll be back in a bit."

The old lady nodded.

On both sides of the property, gates have long strings attached to their latches, threaded through fenceboards. Security is not a priority on Doone Street. Paul reached up and pulled a latch.

No dog appeared. No alarm, no property owner peeking around a corner. A quiet whir came from a four-foot-tall pump, plastic pipes like arteries running day and night to maintain the pool. Other than that, silence.

Paul carried his tools into the backyard. The landlady's skimmer, the shabby broom he had no idea why he'd brought along, it had just seemed lonely. The de-labeled Clorox bottle and a five-gallon bucket of tabs. He still had no idea what they did but they fit the part.

The pool is even cleaner than in its satellite photos. Pristine water shimmies in midday sunlight. A few stray ash leaves pock its surface, like decorative candies tossed as afterthoughts onto a freshly homemade birthday cake. Paul pushed earbuds into his ears; they stretched to his pocket, connected to nothing. It looked the part.

Paul leveled the skimmer. He telescoped its handle for a bit more reach. He tried to focus on the work and block out the two blue Hondas he'd passed coming up the driveway; one had been in the driveway, a CR-V, and the other, an Accord was on the street. Despite the clouds in the sky and predicted rain the cars looked freshly detailed. Tires shone like new. Or maybe no one on Doone ever has cause to dip off a paved road.

"Hello?"

Through the muffle of the earbuds, Paul didn't recognize the voice. But, instinctively, he knew. He kept skimming.

"Excuse me?"

The voice hadn't decided to come thru the sliding glass door yet. Paul imagined what Karen would look like; maybe she'd be wearing a sheer pool cover-up atop a one-piece bathing suit. She'd have the figure of a middle-aged actress who'd taken care of herself, tanned just enough without letting it crepe her skin. She'd have slipped on a pair of sandals. He'd hear them clomping toward him. They'd probably wrap halfway up her calves like those Roman-style things he'd seen.

"Excuse me," the voice was beside him now.

The woman he turned to see was neither lithe in body nor open to whatever shenanigans were going on in her backyard. Karen was not the Karen of a poolman's dreams. Paul heard the skepticism in her voice. Her shoes weren't Roman-esque sandals but the cross-trainers of someone who'd just used a Peloton. She'd looked out her window and hopped right down to confront whoever that guy was cleaning her pool.

He pulled the earbuds from his ears. They fell onto his shoulder.

"Hi!" he said with complete confidence.

"Hi there. Who are you?"

"Paul. And you're Karen."

"Yes. But you're not," she chose her word, "*the* Paul."

"My girlfriend seems to think the same thing. Sometimes she acts like she's waiting for the real Paul to show up, too."

Karen smiled. "No, really. Where's my Paul the Pool Guy?"

Paul scrunched his brow. Like this was the first he was hearing of it.

"I thought I was your Paul the pool guy." He took out his iPhone. He tapped twice and played back her voice, requesting his services.

"Well," she nodded, "that's me. But I usually..."

She took out her own phone. "Ohhh. I see what I did. Paul the Pool Guy's number is here. You must be ... wait. You're saying you're Paul, you're a pool guy, and I called you? Oh! Well, clearly I did because my voice is on your phone."

She eyed him, thinking. She watched him skim.

The moment of truth. His acting skills would sell him or not. He casually, dutifully skimmed the way he imagined a pool guy would. He shifted his buckets aside to reach a cluster of leaves in a corner. He sensed her behind him, making a decision, the way an audience member in a community theatre might decide that the guy in the corner of stage left with the rifle and green fatigues was just enough of a soldier.

"Eh, whatever. Here."

She thrust out her hand, a wad of bills, fives and tens and some ones. Apparently Paul the Pool Guy got cash every week.

He nodded. "Whoa! ATM was out of order this week, eh?"

"Fifty hours a week waitressing. Lucky you're not getting all ones."

Karen sat on a lounge chair, the kind every pool has, with notches in its frame to prop its user like a sundial. "So, Paul the Supposed Pool Guy, what's your story?"

"My story? Which story do you want."

"*The* story. Like, you said something about a girlfriend who doesn't like you."

He skimmed. "It's not that she doesn't like me. It's that I think I've become invisible to her. Like her life is a movie, or a play or something, and I'm just an understudy until the guy who was really cast in the lead shows up."

Karen leaned on an elbow. "That's terrible."

He shrugged. He kept skimming. When his net was full he walked to the brick wall separating the backyard from the narrow city sidewalk. He whacked the tool's shaft on the brick. Real Paul might never do such a thing. But he wasn't here today.

Paul returned to the pool, still in character. He picked up the white plastic bottle and walked along the edge of the water. He titled his wrist and poured his landlady's tap water into the pool.

"How about you," Paul said, "what's your story?"

She sighed. "Don't really have one. Not even a guy who ignores me like your girlfriend. Sorry. That sounded rude. No offense."

"None taken. She does ignore me. Just so we're clear though I don't think she dislikes me. I just think she feels better when certain people aren't around."

"Even you?"

Paul nodded.

"But she must've picked you for some reason," Karen said.

"Maybe she did once. Now I get the feeling she's not sure how to cut me loose. I guess it's kinda fun to watch her squirm." Paul shrugged. "She deserves it. She's the hottest ice queen I've ever seen."

Karen was quiet a moment.

"So what are you doing for dinner tonight, Paul-the-Supposed-Pool Guy?"

Paul carried the empty Clorox bottle to the nearby recycling can, the kind dutiful neighbors carry to their curbs every Wednesday night and dropped it in. He made a mental note to stop by the Dollar Tree and buy the landlady a fresh bottle of bleach.

"Tonight? Nothing. And let me tell you, if you're making an

invite, it couldn't come at a better time because I've been dreaming of a giant steak and plate of potatoes all day. Unless you're *not* making an invitation in which case you'll see me at Taco Bell in about half an hour."

Karen laughed lightly. "I was inviting, but not steak and potatoes. You might have the wrong lady bountiful. I was thinking more like sushi."

"Sushi's even better. I'm already around water all day."

Paul started to wonder when he was going to snap out of this. "What's your favorite place?" He found this a rule with Californians: everyone has their favorite sushi joint, no two people like the same one, and they all believe their place is incapable of doing wrong.

"King Kong Sushi in the Janss Mall. It's not the 'best' place but I like it."

Hearing this bit of humility, Paul pounced. "You're kidding, that's my favorite place! They have that little section on the left of the room - "

Karen interjected "..and they never let..."

".. anyone sit there!" they both said.

"Totally!" she said. She held her palm up which Paul, being male, instinctively high fived.

"So you feel like dining with me, Paul the Supposed Poolguy?"

"Sure, just let me rush home and put on my tux."

"Do you own one?" She'd said it like she almost believed him.

Which made him very, very happy.

———

"You can't do this."

His landlady, Debbie, had a habit of walking in while Paul was getting dressed. It was like living in an episode of *Seinfeld*. At least he had pants on. This time. Today her interest had been aroused when he showed up with a new bottle of Clorox and an old lady in a strange truck.

"Why not," Paul said. "I'm a good guest,. I'll keep my napkin on my lap and chew with my mouth closed."

"It's dishonest."

"Not on any kind of important scale. Did you see who we had as a president?"

"Two wrongs...'" she quoted.

"Don't make Mr. Right, I know. But hey. It's free sushi dinner. With a moderately attractive woman who seems to like me. When's the last time a guy asked you out?"

Debbie simultaneously grimaced and rolled her eyes. "Not the point."

"It isn't?"

"No! What if Shannon finds out."

"Shannon doesn't care."

"Sure she does."

"No. She doesn't."

"Of course she - "

"No, she *doesn't*," Paul interrupted. "Debbie, if she cared I wouldn't feel the way I do. I wouldn't have returned that call today. I wouldn't have taken a day off work, rented a homeless guy's truck with his wife still in it and cleaned a total stranger's pool."

"Why *did* you do that anyway."

Paul thought a moment. "I was bored."

Debbie plopped on the end of his bed and leaned back. He buttoned up a dress shirt. Not his best, but a dress shirt. "Fine. You say she doesn't care. Call Shannon right now and break up with her."

Paul, not in his usual mind, didn't stop to think. He whipped out his cell, scrolled to the S's and tapped.

"Hey. It's me. Look. I'm gonna keep this short. I don't think we should see each other anymore. I don't want to talk about it. Take care."

He tapped. He tossed the phone on the bed.

Debbie sat in silence. She watched the phone. Paul's eyes joined the vigil.

When a full minute had passed, he knew. Debbie knew too. She got off the bed, came over and helped him tighten the knot on his tie.

"Well," she said, "that's two mysteries solved."

He inspected her work. A tie can never be straight enough. "What was the other one?"

She half-smiled. "When I got home my first thought was 'why does my sink smell like Clorox?'"

They laughed. She patted his shoulder. "Have fun."

"Thanks."

"You've earned it."

He reached in his pocket and pulled out the wad of loose bills. She eyed it.

"Just don't go earning any more tonight."

"What kind of gigolo do you take me for? I'm just going to sushi."

"That's how it starts." She patted his shoulders and gave him a gentle push toward the doorway. "Call if you need a ride. You know, when you're making out and her husband-slash-boyfriend-slash-significant other walks in."

"You're such a pessimist."

"Nope, just a fan of threesomes!"

Paul rolled his eyes.

He loved where he lived.

———

Paul took the next three Wednesdays off. He'd borrow the old man's truck and leave the Mazda so regularly that the old man came to expect him. The wife had stopped coming along. He told Paul "I hope you don't mind, she's kinda taken a shining to that little car of yours. We did some errands in it last time."

"That's fine. Zip around town as needed. I'll put you on the insurance."

"Let's not get too comfortable. I think she could get used to something so new and cozy, takes so little gas."

New, Paul thought. The car was a '93. Compared to a '71 Chevy pickup, though, it was practically fresh off the used car lot. "I don't want to be the cause of family strife."

"Oh don't worry. She may get the fever but it breaks pretty quick. Just likes borrowing 'em once in a while. Gives her a fix, guess you could say." The old man rubbed his chin. "I think she's about at the end of her latest bout now."

Paul didn't want to admit it but he and Karen were nearing the end of their bout. The first two weeks were a hot love affair. Just what he needed. He imagined she enjoyed telling girlfriends she was sleeping with the pool boy.

On that fourth Wednesday, he pulled up to 96 Doone to see a pickup at the curb, sporting a magnetic sign on its door. *Paul's Pool Service*. A weekly dash of tap water could only keep algae at bay so long. Paul restarted the old man's truck and went back to Debbie's house. He put the tools and the chlorine tabs back where they belonged and took a nap. Around sundown, he returned to the old man's corner.

"How was work today?"

Paul traded the truck key for his own. "Got laid off."

"Bah."

"Nothing good lasts forever."

"Boy, got that right. Shame it has to change when you get something good going."

"It was fun while it was going, though."

"I guess the question is, now what do you do?"

"Back to the box factory. Kiss and make up with the girlfriend. This was a nice little diversion, but ..."

"Yeah. Well, sometimes a little diversion's all we need to keep ourselves sane. Until the next time we need a little diversion."

"Yeah."

"Well, if you ever need the truck again..."

"And if the wifey needs to go out and do errands in style..."

"Will do." The old man gave a two-finger salute from the tip of his cap.

Paul walked to the parking lot where the Mazda and the old man's truck stood side by side. He caught the old lady's eye. She waved. Paul waved back. Then he got in the Mazda and twisted its key.

He'd just checked his mirrors and was about to put the car in gear when he spotted a familiar car – Shannon's. Only she wasn't driving it. She sat in the passenger seat. A man he'd never met steered them through the lot, toward a parking spot in front of the bank.

Paul couldn't help himself.

He watched them park and go into the building. Paul walked in like any other customer. He went to the customer's counter, the one with the deposit and withdrawal slips; he picked one up and picked up a pen. What would a customer do? He scribbled on a deposit slip *what is she doing* and *gee Paul, you're so easily replaced.* Soon a man in a suit came up to the desk where they'd been waiting and greeted them with handshakes.

"Mister and Misses Scott," said the loan officer.

Jesus Christ, that was fast.

Paul kept scribbling at the self-service desk. He crumpled the slip he'd been writing on, grimaced as if having made a mistake, then picked up a fresh slip and put the pen to it. He made out a deposit for ten million dollars. His back turned, over the scratching of the pen he heard:

"... reviewed your application..."

"... appropriate level of annual combined income..."

"... years employed and married..."

".... congratulations."

It was the last word that resonated inside him, like an echo in a grand canyon. He let it bounce around. Finally, he was glad to have been the one to break it off.

He couldn't wait to get home. He would call Babe and tell him about the bank. Chances were his friend had known all along.

Paul would time his arrival with the hour Debbie was due from work. He'd hear her car pull up. Then he'd turn on the shower, long and hot, and wait until she interrupted. He imagined reaching thru the shower curtain and giving her wrist a little tug.

Then he snapped out of the illusion. Tonight was her bowling night. And, he realized, it was the first Wednesday after the theatre's latest show had opened.

Auditions would be tonight.

He started the car. He was practiced. Willing.

Ready.

LOST

DAVID LANGE

"Swipe left on that one. Ew, that one, too."

"Why should I dump her?" asked Mitchell, "she looks nice."

"Dude? Seriously? Are you looking for a date or someone to instruct you on the finer points of the Dewey Decibel System?"

"Decimal."

"What?"

"Decimal. The Dewey Decimal System. That's what you meant to say."

"Whatever...you can do better than that, Mitchell," chided Sasha. "Look, if you go into settings and then filters, you can sort chicks by their bust size. That's a good starting point." Charlie shot Sasha a nasty glance across the table where the three friends were seated.

"Don't mind Sasha," said Charlie, "he has a one-track mind. If you want to date a girl with a small chest then more power to you—someone's got to give us flat-chested gals a chance."

"Hey, Charlie, let me do the coaching here. You know you'd be the first in line for a boob job if you could afford it," kidded Sasha. Charlie wasn't amused.

"Would you guys just stop it!" exclaimed Mitchell. "I'm not going to sort for chest size. That's not what I'm looking for."

"You could have fooled me," said Charlie. "The last girl you dated was packing some monsters."

"Yah, what did you do to screw that one up, Mitchell," added Sasha.

"I didn't screw it up. I don't know what I did. She posted a few swimsuit photos of herself on Facebook and I clicked "LIKE" instead of clicking on the "LOVE" button and she took that as an insult to her person."

"More like an insult to her plastic surgeon," laughed Charlie.

"And then I guess I was supposed to text her every morning to tell her I love her and then, again, each night to remind her that she's the most beautiful girl in the universe."

"What? You didn't message her at least twice a day? No wonder she dumped you," said Charlie.

"How the heck was I supposed to know I was supposed to text her two dozen times a day to tell her she was God's gift to the human race and that Venus paled in comparison."

"You've got a lot to learn about women," said Charlie.

"Says the girl who goes by a guy's name." Mitchell immediately regretted his unkind remark.

"Yah, nice comeback, Clueless Joe."

"Sorry, Shar-leeen. Did I offend your fine sensibilities?"

"Hey, chill out love birds," interrupted Sasha. "We've got to find Mitchell a new squeeze and I'm thinking we can find a suitable prospect on Hot One Dot Com before the evening's out. Hey! Here's a promising candidate. Five-six, blonde hair, blue eyes, and look at that killer bod!"

"Did this one at least graduate from high school?" asked Charlie.

"Look at that figure! I don't care if she made it past pre-K."

"We're all familiar with your taste in women, Sasha, but remember Mitchell is looking for his Turner Classic Movies dream girl."

"Hey! What's that supposed to mean, Charlie?" asked Mitchell. Charlie ignored Mitchell's query and reached over to grab Mitchell's cell phone from Sasha who had been rapidly scrolling through the dating site's profile photos with lust-driven enthusiasm.

"Oh, come on Sasha! This pic has been filtered and Photoshopped and God only knows what else. Look, zero freckles, zero skin blemishes and...oh...oh my God...check this out..."

"What?" asked Sasha. "Looks fine to me."

"If you can force your eyes to look beyond the cleavage, you might notice her ankles accidentally got Photoshopped away. Sloppy, sloppy, sloppy."

"So, what are you saying, Charlie?" asked Mitchell. "Do you think that maybe she really isn't a Princeton graduate and founder and CEO of a highly successful cosmetics company?"

"Well, I wouldn't be surprised if she sold some nail polish on the flea market circuit but, at this point, I'm not putting a lot of stock in anything on that profile. Swipe left and save yourself some pain, my friend."

"Gone." With a flick of his index finger, Mitchell sent Gia Giambianni back into the dating pool, confident that her inbox would soon be overflowing with fish attracted to the bikini-clad bait she had graciously cast into the sea of frenzied, sex-starved, suitors. "She's going to make a great "ex" for some business mogul looking for eye candy to take to the annual holiday party," thought Mitchell. "I wish the happy couple luck."

Mitchell Barry was well beyond cynical. Several months of online dating services, speed dating events, blind dates, and singles social gatherings had left him convinced that not only were all "the good ones" taken but that anyone who remained was either a shameless gold-digger or emotionally and/or mentally damaged beyond repair. He was also quite sure that any woman that would be a possible match for him would, likewise, assume the worst of any of the males remaining in the dating pool. It was so depressing. "I guess you've got one shot at young love," he thought, "and if you don't get that right then you're cursed for life."

"Hey. Hey! Earth to Mitchell. Are you there, Mitchell?" said

Charlie, waking him from his dreamy trance.

"What? Did you and Sasha find me another winner? Does this one have ankles?"

"Over there, Tiger King. The pretty Asian girl at the corner table has been eyeing you these past five minutes."

"What? Really?"

"Stop! Don't look. Be cool, dude."

"So, explain to me why I shouldn't look at her, Charlie."

"You've got to play it cool. If you scamper over like some love-sick puppy, you'll shoot yourself in the foot before you ever get out the first hello."

"Okay, Doctor Lovehart, relationship oracle, how should I play this?"

"So, here's what you do. First, lose that nerdy windbreaker and borrow Sasha's leather trench coat. Next, make like you're heading to the bathroom and give 'em your best sexy smile as you pass by. Slick down that hair with some water in the men's room and comb it back. When you come out, saunter over and ask if you can buy the table some drinks. Speak to the group but lock eyes with the girl who's been ogling you this whole time. If things work out, you can tell us the story tomorrow morning. You've got protection, right?"

"Whoa, whoa, whoa! Don't you think it'd be better if I maybe asked the girl for her phone number first? Maybe go on a date or two? And, another thing, what's wrong with my jacket. It happens to be very functional and I really like it."

"It happens to be very dorky," Sasha chimed in, "and if you wear that, you won't have to worry about 'protection' because you'll never get past first base. Here, take my coat but please don't soil it—I'm not sure your weekly salary would cover the professional cleaning cost for this garment."

"Oh, be nice," said Charlie. "Mitchell is all but guaranteed to get promoted before this year is out."

"Yah, promoted to Assistant Deputy Administrator for Lost Paperwork. That'll change his life trajectory, for sure."

"Hey, buddy, why don't you show a little love here and stop beating up on your friend who is already battling the demons of low self-esteem and general hopelessness."

"Sorry, dude. I'm just messing with you. You know that, right?"

"Yah, I know, Sasha. I'm just a little sensitive these days. Also, I can't help but think that I'll be more likely to find a girl of interest to me if I just...well, you know...just be myself."

"You can be yourself once the wedding vows are done, my friend. Until then, your best shot is actually dressing like an adult and at least pretending to be a little suaver than Charlie Brown."

"Swell. Now that you've pumped me up with that great pep talk, why don't you toss that coat over here so I can go and make a complete fool of myself."

"Hey, Mitchell, if you're going to be a fool then try to be the best fool ever," added Charlie.

"I'm halfway there, already, Charlie. Save my drink, I'll be back in a nanosecond."

Mitchell reluctantly donned the long leather coat and walked towards the Men's Room, mindful of his posture and his gait. He quickly glanced over at the corner table and winked at the girls, leaving them giggling as he passed by. In the bathroom, he ran his comb under the faucet and then combed his hair back. "Ridiculous! I look absolutely freakin' ridiculous." The new look definitely felt unnatural but rather than endure the ridicule of his tablemates, he decided to carry on with the plan.

After a final check in the mirror, Mitchell took a deep breath, exhaled, and made his way out of the Men's Room, heading for the table in the corner. He could feel his stomach muscles tightening as he drew closer.

"Hey, how you ladies doin'?" asked Mitchell, speaking to the group but focused on the attractive Asian girl who had been watching him. Once again, the girls giggled and looked toward one another.

"Oh, we're doing great," said Susan, a lovely Korean-American law student with model-perfect long black hair, a perfect complexion, and impossibly angelic brown eyes. "I'm Susan," she said, "and these are my friends Astrid and Charna." She reached out her hand in greeting and Mitchell, trying to be suaver than Charlie Brown, took her hand and gently kissed it, just as he had seen done in the old-time romantic movies that he loved. Susan blushed and the girls all laughed.

"Smooth move, Don Juan," said Charna, an attractive red-head with an accent that Mitchell was unable to place. At that moment, Mitchell realized that he probably would have been better served to have simply shaken Susan's hand. He was confused. Mitchell knew he was anything but a Don Juan.

"Would you care to join us for some drinks," asked Susan. "That is if your friends over there won't miss you too much. That's not your girlfriend, is it?"

"Oh, Charlie? No. I've known Sasha and Charlie since grade school and they're just my buddies."

"Oh, good," said Astrid, an evil grin forming on her face. The tone of her voice sent shivers through Mitchell's body. He looked back to his table and Charlie and Sasha laughed as they both gave him a big thumbs up from across the room.

"Actually, I'm pretty sure my friends are glad to be rid of me. I'd love to join you ladies for a drink." Mitchell flagged down the wandering waitress and collected orders from the group. While Susan continued her role as the ice-breaking queen, Mitchell could not help but feel like he had been lured into the age-old "bait and switch" trap. Astrid's gaze remained excruciatingly fixed upon him as if she were some cat stalking her prey in the garden. Astrid's professionally crafted coiffure seemed impossibly gravity-defying while her perfume, a mysterious blend of rare fruits and spices from the lesser-known regions of Southeast Asia, overpowered even the aroma of deep-fried onion rings and chicken strips that permeated the majority of the establishment.

"Love your coat," said Astrid. "It's really sexy and suits you well."

The coat, in fact, did not suit Mitchell at all. Not only was it two sizes too large but he was pretty certain the coat was better suited for the lead character from a 1970s blacksploitation film.

"Hi, I'm John Shaft," joked Mitchell.

"Hi, John! I'm Astrid. It's wonderful to meet you." The wind created by the flapping of Astrid's oversized batting false eyelashes nearly knocked Mitchell out of his seat. Clearly, Astrid had never seen *Shaft*, nor any of its sequels, and his joke was lost into the void of attempted humor that failed to connect with intended recipients. He sighed.

"Sorry, I was joking. My name is actually Mitchell."

"Oh, you're such a kidder, Mitchell," said Astrid. "Hey, hand me your phone, gorgeous. I want to Air Fling you my phone number."

"You want to do what?" Mitchell had no idea what Astrid was talking about.

"Air Fling, silly. So that you have me in your contacts." Mitchell was not at all sure that he wanted to relinquish his phone to his new acquaintance but, with all eyes upon him, he buckled under the pressure and sheepishly handed his cell phone over to Astrid. In a blur of motion, Astrid's exquisitely manicured, passion-red painted nails tapped furiously upon the touchscreen of his phone. Somewhere in there, Mitchell was fairly certain he had heard the tell-tale dot-dot-dot, dash-dash-dash, dot-dot-dot that was Morse code for S-O-S. "Almost done, lover," added Astrid, her gaze fixed upon Mitchell's cell phone. Mitchell would have been taken aback, being called "lover" by a stranger, but he was too fixated upon the elaborate makeup scheme adorning the painted doll sitting across from him. He wondered how many layers were built up upon the foundation and he speculated what the creature below looked like in her natural state. To be honest, he much preferred natural-looking women to their "photoshoot" versions but he willingly accepted the milder varieties of tribal cosmetology.

"Done!" exclaimed Astrid, looking over toward Mitchell and expecting a facial reaction that would betray his elation and immeasurable joy. Mitchell did his best to fake a satisfied smile. "I'm in your contacts now and I also made us Facebook friends. You really need to get yourself a Twitter account, Instagram, TikTok, and..." Mitchell was still unhappy about the fact that Astrid had usurped his cell phone and so he missed the ongoing discussion regarding the many other social media sites that he was supposed to belong to as an evolved hominid living in the 21st Century.

"Okay. Thanks, Astrid," mumbled Mitchell. He wanted to lash out but he really didn't have it in him to be cruel. Besides this, it'd been so long since any girl had been so enthusiastic about him that he was helplessly lured like a moth to the flame.

"Excuse me," said Astrid, "but I've got to go pee-pee. Too many Margaritas." The other girls laughed and raised their glasses as if to toast. Meanwhile, Mitchell was still coming to grips with the term "pee-pee" which he had only previously heard in the context of toddler potty training and dog park guidance to pets. Astrid got up and began to saunter toward the Ladies Room, her earrings clanging like Tibetan wind chimes.

While Astrid was gussying herself up in the Ladies Room, Mitchell continued conversing with Susan and Charna. He really liked Susan and was disappointed to find out that she had a steady boyfriend. He wasn't surprised. It seemed that all the smart, beautiful, and intellectually interesting women were already spoken for. Mitchell found Charna to be rather intriguing, as well, but, through the course of their conversation, it came to light that Charna preferred members of her own sex. So, it looked like Astrid was the only game in town that night. Mitchell steeled himself for the reappearance of Astrid. He looked briefly over at his friends who appeared to be mobilizing for their departure. Sasha queried Mitchell from across the room with a thumbs up and thumbs down hand gesture. Mitchell nodded, indicating he was going to stick this one out and his friends responded with a salute and wave as they got up from their table. He was on his own now. His cell phone vibrated in his pocket. He asked the girls to excuse him as he looked at his text message, expecting to see some snide remark from Sasha or Charlie. Instead, he was greeted by a text from his new Facebook friend, Astrid. Her text message read simply, "Do you miss me yet?" Was Astrid texting him from the bathroom stall? He stared at the screen, confused. Clicking on a smiley face emoji was the best he could come up with to respond to the message from Astrid. What had he gotten himself into?

Astrid returned, shortly thereafter, with a few extra splashes of perfume, for good measure, and an extra layer of lipstick upon her impossibly red lips. Mitchell assumed it was no accident that Astrid's blouse was unbuttoned two inches lower than it was previously. He tried not to stare. Astrid seemed disappointed and readjusted her position, concerned that the target of her mating displays had somehow missed the signals she was firing like flares into the night sky.

The evening wore on and Mitchell became less enchanted with Astrid as the effects of the alcohol began to wear off. His Jeep was in the lot of the shopping center across the street and he fully intended to drive himself home that night. As such, he transitioned to soft drinks as the girls continued to call for beverages at the table. Each time Mitchell began to enjoy his conversation with Susan or Charna, Astrid would attempt to contribute to the discussion and lower the Intelligence Quotient of the discussion by a full forty points. For all that, he retained his civility and reminded himself that intellectual prowess was only one attribute of many terrific facets that made partners desirable. He convinced himself that he'd much rather be dating a dull but kind woman than a brilliant villainess with evil intent. He smiled as he thought about various attractive Bond movie villainesses but was awoken from his daydreaming when Astrid reached over to hold his hand.

"I think I've probably had enough to drink tonight. Would you mind taking me home, Mitch?" asked Astrid. Mitchell looked over toward Susan and then to Charna.

"Astrid's running a hot yoga session tomorrow morning at the

Tranquility Healing & Wellness Center," said Charna, "so she needs to get tucked in for the night. Susan and I are probably going to hang out a little longer, so why don't you two love birds run along."

"I could maybe call an Uber?" offered Mitchell, squirming to extract himself from the unwanted commitment.

"You'd put a drunk girl in an Uber at this time of night?" queried an incredulous Susan. Mitchell knew she was right but he felt like he was getting boxed into a moral corner and he didn't appreciate the manipulation.

"No. You're right. I'll take Astrid home."

"See, I told you he was a gentleman," said Charna to Susan.

"Don't be too much of a gentleman," added Astrid with a sly smile. The girls all laughed as Mitchell's discomfort level elevated from "danger-danger" to "get me the heck out of here, NOW!"

After winding down their conversation, Mitchell bid farewell to Susan and Charna and escorted Astrid out of the club. Astrid took his arm affectionately, but also to help stabilize herself as she was still feeling rather drunk. Distracted by Astrid's incessant chattering, Mitchell completely forgot where he had parked his car in the shopping center. Feeling somewhat embarrassed, he had to double back and search several rows of parked vehicles, all the while Astrid was poking fun at his sense of direction. That meant a lot, coming from a woman who could barely walk, let alone help to find a vehicle in a dimly lit parking lot. For all that, Mitchell walked confidently and felt like he was somehow fulfilling a chivalrous duty by escorting his charge back to her apartment. Filled with purpose, Mitchell seemed satisfied to know that at least two intoxicated women felt that he was a more reliable protector for their friend than a random Uber car service driver. That was a true compliment. He chuckled to himself as he considered the ridiculous events of the evening.

After several erroneous turn directions provided by his lovesick companion, Mitchell finally arrived at Astrid's apartment complex. He stopped the vehicle but left the engine running as he walked around to open Astrid's door.

"Oh my God, you are such a gentleman," gushed Astrid, stumbling on her words. She took Mitchell's hand as he helped her out of the vehicle. Astrid barely took a stride before stumbling and nearly falling. She steadied herself and then fumbled through her purse beneath the nearby lamp post until she found her keys. "Would you mind?"

Mitchell's brow furrowed and he sighed deeply before returning to his vehicle to turn the engine off. As much as he just wanted the evening to end, he couldn't bear the thought of leaving only to have Astrid topple over and do a face plant on the sidewalk. He resumed his escort duties, and none too soon—Astrid literally fell into his arms, laughing hysterically.

"I didn't think I had that much tonight. You slipped something into my drink, didn't you, you sly dog?"

"No, Astrid. I didn't put anything in your drink. Now let's get you into your apartment so you can sleep this off."

"Carry me."

"I'm not going to carry you, Astrid. Now, please, let's just get you inside." Astrid made a pouty face and wrapped her arms around Mitchell's neck before giving him a kiss on the lips.

While the sensation was nice, Mitchell did not enjoy inhaling Astrid's alcohol-infused breath. Worse yet, he imagined her layers of lipstick transferring to his own lips.

"There's more where that came from, lover," said the amorous yet barely conscious Astrid. Mitchell did not reply but continued leading Astrid toward her apartment. He felt a sense of relief once inside the door and off the well-lit stage of the apartment complex's lot. After turning on the lights, he was nearly blinded by the brilliant explosion of neon pink. Pink everywhere! Pink and cats. "Now, there's a creative theme," he thought. Cat wall clocks, cat posters, cat pillows, cat dish towels, cat everything.

"Looks like you really love cats, Astrid."

"You already knew that from my Facebook page, silly." Mitchell, in fact, had neither the time nor the desire to investigate Astrid's

Facebook page; a page he had only received access to, thanks to Astrid's intervention, a few hours earlier.

"So, where's your cat? Waiting to pounce on strangers?"

"Oh, I can't have cats. I'm terribly allergic to them. They make me break out in really ugly red blotches...and then there's that horrible coughing and wheezing."

"Yikes! Sorry about that. Well, it seems you've got a few dozen stuffed animal cats on your bed to help keep you company."

"Would you like to join us?"

"While rolling around in the sack with you and your pride of plush felines sounds like a dream come true, I think I'll pass tonight."

"Oh, please don't leave me. You're making me so sad. I think I'm going to cry," pouted Astrid.

"I really ought to be going and you really need to get some sleep."

"Can you help me with my shoes?" said Astrid, as she fell back upon her bed, kicking her feet into the air. Mitchell considered the task. The extravagant high-heeled sandals were purposely selected to highlight Astrid's hundred-dollar pedicure. She kicked her feet about, frolicking in her bed.

"I'm pretty sure you can get those by yourself, Astrid."

"No, I can't. I'm too drunk. You've got to help me. I'll never get any sleep with these shoes on."

Mitchell was fairly sure that Astrid would soon be sound asleep, even if she were wearing ski boots, but he thought a final act of kindness might pave the way for his departure. "Shoes and then I'm going."

"You're a dear. Don't be looking up my dress while you're busy down there."

"Hold still, please," said Mitchell, desperately fumbling with a completely unfamiliar and ridiculously petite ankle strap and buckle system. With Astrid squirming about, restlessly, the task proved much more challenging than he had imagined and he nearly got kicked in the face more than once.

"Do you like the nails? Got them done just this morning. Cost me nearly a hundred."

"Really? I would have guessed three-hundred or better," said Mitchell, having absolutely no idea what a professional pedicure cost and dumbfounded that anyone would invest more than twenty bucks to do something they could easily do themselves, or so he believed. Astrid laughed.

"Three-hundred? Where do you go to get your nails done that cost three hundred dollars? I want some of that."

"Look, Astrid, I'm having a really difficult time with these shoes. Could you, maybe, hold still for just a few seconds?"

Mitchell returned to the task at hand or, more precisely, at foot, but was immediately distracted by flashes of light. He looked over and saw Astrid grinning as she snapped photos on her cell phone of Mitchell attempting to unbuckle her sandals.

"What the hell! Stop that! Give me your phone, Astrid!"

"You can't have my phone. It's mine. Now get back to work and then you can help me with the dress."

"Okay. I'm out of here. Have a good night, Astrid."

"Wait," responded Astrid, now tearing up. "I didn't mean to make you angry. I was just playing around." Mitchell gently swung Astrid's feet back over to the bed and he stood up. "Please stay."

"I've got to go. I've got an early day tomorrow and so do you."

"No, I don't," responded Astrid.

"Hot yoga. Remember?"

"Oh, that. I'll just call in sick. Please spend the night. I'll treat you to breakfast at McDonald's in the morning."

"Good night, Astrid." Mitchell turned around and left the bedroom. He could hear Astrid's nearly incoherent whaling voice following him to the door, as he made his way out. After closing the door, he quickly headed for his vehicle. He dreaded the thought of Astrid following him so he quickly started the car and put it in reverse. Unfortunately, he wasn't quite fast enough. As he was backing out, Astrid appeared at the entrance to her apartment, makeup smeared, only one shoe on, and clearly despondent.

"Call me, tomorrow. Please, call me tomorrow!" she shouted. Mitchell felt extremely embarrassed as several lights came on across the apartment complex, residents peering across the lot to see what all the commotion was about. Opening his car window, he gave a friendly wave to Astrid as he drove into the darkness.

The next morning, Mitchell woke, exhausted. The events of the evening were still weighing on his mind. "Maybe Astrid is okay when she's sober?" he thought. "At least she liked me. But, she's not exactly what I've been looking for. In fact, I'm not even sure what it is I'm looking for anymore." Mitchell wiped the sleep from his eyes and steeled himself for his usual morning routine—social media and news check, shower, shave, and assorted bathroom activities. With groggy eyes, he tried to focus on his cell phone and noticed a message from his friend, Charlie. She wrote, "Looks like somebody made a big impression last night!" What did that mean? Upon further inspection of his social media page, he noticed that his last Facebook post had been acknowledged with a "LOVE" response by Astrid. She "LOVED" his previous post, as well. And the one before that. In fact, as Mitchell scrolled back along his timeline in Facebook, he was horrified to see that Astrid had "LOVED" every single post and every single photo of him going back at least two years. The thought that she had spent all night haunting his Facebook page was very alarming to Mitchell. "This is Fatal Attraction kind of stuff," he thought to himself. Mitchell returned his phone to its charging stand and went to the bathroom for his shower.

Still distracted by the strange turn of events, Mitchell accidentally cut himself while shaving. He cursed under his breath and blamed Astrid for his woes. He blamed himself, too. Mitchell had reluctantly dipped his toe back into the dating pool and he had hardly gotten wet before he was plagued by second thoughts. Putting a little bandage upon his cheek, he dressed in his work clothes and returned to collect his wristwatch and cell phone. The phone had four messages waiting for him—all from Astrid. Each was a slight variation of the common theme— "I think we have real chemistry and

I can't wait to see you again. Call me as soon as you can and let's set something up." Mitchell didn't respond immediately. He thought it prudent to carefully consider the matter before moving forward. Meanwhile, Sasha was texting him to ask if he "got lucky with the blonde last night." Despite the urge to remain glued to the screen, Mitchell set his phone to vibrate and headed out to his car.

Passing McDonald's on his way to work, Mitchell laughed to himself, envisioning what the romantic breakfast at McDonald's that Astrid had suggested the night before might have looked like. While he was driving, his cell phone kept vibrating in his pocket. Someone seemed very anxious to get a hold of him and he feared an emergency at his parents' home. As such, Mitchell pulled off onto the shoulder and pulled out his phone. Astrid! Three text messages and one voice mail stating that she thought he would have contacted her by now. Frustrated, Mitchell returned the phone to his pocket and continued on to work. Rather than make an uncomfortable matter even more difficult, Mitchell decided to call Astrid from the parking lot at work. Astrid seemed annoyed at the "lack of communication" but quickly shifted to a sunnier disposition.

"So, Mitch, I've been thinking. I know you've probably got some great plans baking in the oven right now, but I thought I'd help us along so I went and bought two tickets to the X-Ray Bandits concert this Tuesday. I thought that maybe we could go out to dinner before the concert, see the show, and then, well, you know, maybe hang out a bit." Mitchell immediately regretted initiating contact with her only fifteen minutes before he was supposed to begin a productive day of work.

"Astrid, I really wish you would have asked me first before you went ahead and purchased those tickets. I mean, how would you even know if I'm free that night?"

"You are free though, aren't you?" asked Astrid, in a frightening tone that somehow gave Mitchell the idea that Astrid already knew his schedule. There was a part of Mitchell that wanted to take the easy road and simply lie about his availability. That's what most of his friends would have done. However, he valued his integrity too much to fib, even under such dire circumstances.

"I think so," he meekly replied. "I'm just not sure I want to go to a concert on Tuesday night. It's a work day and…"

"Well, I have to work, too," interrupted Astrid. "I'll tell you what, I'll make sure you're back in your bed before you turn into a pumpkin, okay?"

"Who the heck are X-Ray Bandits, anyway?"

"Are you serious? Dude, I need to get you out more and expand your horizons. They're only the top-rated New Age Goth Band in Suffolk County. Duh. You're going to love them." Mitchell's cell phone dinged and he was hoping it was a matter that would provide his excuse to drop the conversation with Astrid. "Did you get it?"

"Get what?" inquired Mitchell.

"I just gifted you the most recent X-Ray Bandits album on iTunes. You know, as a warm-up for our date Tuesday night."

"Look, Astrid, allow me to be more direct here. I do not want to go to a concert on Tuesday night. Maybe we could go for a drink at the club again, sometime. Or I could take you out for coffee?"

"What?! A coffee get-together? You're treating me like a stranger all of a sudden and it hurts."

"Hey, I'm sorry Astrid. I didn't want to hurt you. I just think maybe we should slow things down a little bit and…" Just then, a few of Mitchell's co-workers rapped on his car window and pointed to their watches while having a laugh. "Astrid, I've got to go but I'll talk to you again soon."

"Wait! We're not done yet. Don't you dare hang up on me, Mitchell!"

"Sorry. I've got to go." Mitchell ended the call and returned the phone to his pocket before opening the car door and sliding out of his seat. His co-workers teased him about waiting until the very last second before clocking in for his shift at the customer service hub.

With a sigh, Mitchell plopped down into his uncomfortable office chair within a sterile, distraction-free, cubicle. Phones began ringing nearly immediately and he launched into customer service mode. All the while, his cell phone continued to vibrate on its charging pad. His employer looked unfavorably upon anyone using their personal cell phones in the office, unless they were on break, so Mitchell resisted the urge to find out what was going on. He wasn't even ten seconds into his first break period before he grabbed his phone off the charger and investigated the recent activity. On his Facebook profile, Astrid had, in an act of immature retribution, converted all the heart emoji "LOVE" responses to his posts and photos to the angry-faced "ANGRY" emojis.

Heading to the bathroom, he ran into his friend Brad. Brad was a tech wiz and worked in his company's IT Department.

"Hey, Brad, I've got a tech question for you."

"Whoa, whoa, Mitchell. I'm off the clock for another seven minutes."

"Dude? Seriously?"

"No. I'm just messing with you, Mitch. What's bugging you—having trouble with getting your streaming TV channels? WIFI devices not connecting at home?"

"Cell phone calendars."

"What about them?" asked Brad, intrigued and always interested in displaying his technical prowess to his co-workers.

"Is it possible for someone to hack into your personal schedule on your cell phone?"

"iPhone?"

"Yes."

"Very unlikely unless they were a real pro. Apple's pretty good about security."

"Whew, I'm really glad to hear that," said a relieved Mitchell.

"Why, do you think someone is messing with your calendar?"

"I guess not. I just let this girl borrow my cell phone last night for a few minutes and now..."

"You did what?!" exclaimed Brad. "You gave physical control of your mobile device to an unknown party?"

"She was just supposed to Air Fling me her contact information, Brad. That's all."

"And is that all she did?"

"Well. No. She made us Facebook friends and..." Brad interrupted Mitchell in mid-sentence.

"And how long, exactly, did she have control of your phone?"

"I don't know. Just a few minutes, I think."

"A few minutes?! Mitchell, you knucklehead, she could have gained access to your contacts, your schedule, your email correspondence, and even your bank account and credit card information in that time. What were you thinking?!"

"I. I don't know. I figured we'd just exchange contact information."

"Next time, maybe consider a business card."

"Right. A business card for dating? Nice. Do you actually ever get out, Brad?" Looking a bit offended, Brad reached into his pocket and pulled out his phone. With a couple of taps, his screen filled with the image of a very attractive Indian-American woman who could easily have been a model.

"My girlfriend," said Brad, proudly. "A Harvard grad." Mitchell was left momentarily speechless and his tonic immobility was all the response that his co-worker needed to close the discussion with an exclamation. Mitchell felt even more inadequate than he had before. Guys in IT were scoring the cream of the crop on the dating scene while he was doing his best to fend off psychopaths and deeply embittered women with insurmountable trust issues.

"She's gorgeous, Brad." Brad nodded, content that his point had been made.

"Don't lend out your electronic devices, my friend. That's just asking for trouble."

"I know. I just wasn't anticipating this ditsy blonde to be the agent of some kind of cyber-attack."

"They're the worst kind, Mitchell. You never see it coming and then, BAM, you're hacked."

"Do you think that, maybe, you could take a quick look?"

"And now I have three minutes remaining on my break," said Brad, somewhat annoyed. But Brad was a good man and, despite his personality quirks, he was always there to help.

"Maybe later, then?"

"Let me take a look."

"You want me to surrender my phone to you?" joked Mitchell.

"Very good. You're learning. Now, the phone, please." Mitchell handed Brad his phone and he went into the phone's email and scheduling permissions to inspect the damage. "Hmm. Interesting."

"What?" inquired Mitchell.

"Nicely done. Just a few minutes, you say?"

"Yah. Two to three tops."

"You are currently sharing your email, contacts, and calendar with HotAstrid98's iPhone."

"Damn it! That bitch!" Mitchell was furious.

"Settle down, my friend. A couple of clicks and a swipe and, voila, you're a free man again."

"I can't thank you enough, Brad. You rock!"

"Oh, you don't have to thank me. I'm going out with Ananya on Tuesday night. I don't need any more boosts to my self-esteem."

"Concert?"

"Yes, nice guess. Wait, you haven't hacked into my calendar, have you?" Brad asked with a chuckle.

"X-Ray Bandits?"

"Oh my God, you have hacked me!" Mitchell just winked and laughed. He pulled his cell phone out of Brad's hand and gave him a wave as he turned for the men's room.

"Enjoy your night out with Ananya," he added as he was walking away.

"You can count on it, Mitchell. Yes, you can be sure about that one."

After taking care of business in the Men's Room, Mitchell returned to his desk and immediately "unfriended" and "blocked"

Astrid on Facebook. The only thing he struggled with was whether or not he even wanted to send her a text to express his anger over being tricked into allowing Astrid to gain permission to private features on his cell phone. One way or the other, he was done with her so he didn't feel like it really mattered. His break was over and calls were, once again, being routed to his desk. Mitchell found it very hard to concentrate as his mind was still occupied by the Astrid situation. More than one customer expressed their frustration as they had to repeat their concerns multiple times to the distracted agent. To make matters worse, his phone was vibrating like mad on the charging pad, yet again. He could resist the temptation no longer and so, contrary to company policy, he removed his work headset and left his phone off the hook while he investigated the happenings on his personal phone.

Astrid had hardly been blocked more than ten or fifteen minutes before she sent a number of angry text messages to Mitchell, accusing him of a bitter betrayal, failed integrity, and a host of other crimes and misdemeanors. He didn't even bother to listen to the voicemail traffic from Astrid.

Of greater concern were several texts from his friends, Sasha and Charlie. Sasha joked about a foot fetish prince looking for his Cinderella while Charlie offered some more constructive recommendations about checking his Facebook settings and changing the photo tagging feature to require his approval before any posts appeared on his Facebook timeline. "What are they are talking about?" Mitchell wondered. He went to his profile page, on Facebook, and things immediately became clear. Someone named Cuddlefish98 had posted several photos from the night before of him attempting to unbuckle Astrid's sandals while she lay in bed. He knew, immediately, that Astrid must have friended him with her alternate profile as well as her primary Facebook profile. Mitchell turned beet red and pounded his fist on his desk, in anger. Right on cue, his team manager poked his head into the cubicle.

"Mitchell, could I talk with you in my office, please."

"I'm sorry, Mr. Brannon. I was just having a moment."

"If you were focusing on work rather than on private matters on your personal cell phone, I think you might find there'd be fewer of those moments in your day. Now, if you wouldn't mind, please follow me to my office."

The call center went strangely quiet as Mitchell stormed out, a pink slip in his hand and uttering a stream of profanity that was becoming all too familiar within those workspaces. He had been canned. It wasn't even about the desk pounding or the cell phone usage. His customer service rating had fallen from 4.2 stars to 2.5 stars. With countless drones waiting in the wings, Mitchell's drop in performance was all the incentive his boss needed to make the personnel change.

Sitting alone in his vehicle, Mitchell turned his satellite radio to a classical music station hoping that the soothing notes might somehow slow his racing heartbeat. He fidgeted anxiously, trapped in the head-space that existed somewhere between a primal yell and melancholy sobbing. Returning to his Facebook page, he deleted the posts that were attracting comments like ants to a picnic. He then blocked Cuddlefish98 on Facebook and began the laborious process of removing any friend he was not familiar with. There were too many. How did he get 3,543 Facebook friends in the first place? Finally, exasperated, embarrassed, and emotionally exhausted, he decided to simply delete his entire Facebook account. And just like that, it was gone. 3,543 friends and probably only three or four real friends in the bunch. This desperate act proved to be very satisfying. Mitchell felt as if a burden had been lifted almost immediately. He turned his cell phone off and tossed it on the passenger seat.

The scenery on his drive seemed, somehow, more colorful and vibrant than he had ever recalled seeing though he had driven the route hundreds of times. Rather than going directly home, Mitchell changed his route to take him through his childhood hometown. He parked in the lot of his favorite childhood park and turned off the car engine. Mitchell looked out upon the water, for a while, before getting out to walk around. He spent nearly an hour at the water's edge before deciding to continue his explorations beyond the gates of the park. His mind adrift in a sea of memories, he walked familiar roads that took him by his former schools, his old house, and finally to his beloved library. He felt ashamed that he hadn't read a book in over three years. He used to love reading.

Mitchell walked into the familiar main lobby of the library and compared the scene to a simpler time when the building radiated with infinite possibilities and his adventures within this enchanted palace seemed infinite and sublimely magical. Like all things, the establishment had evolved with the times. Cumbersome photographic checkout machines were replaced by barcode scanning wands at the checkout desks and computer terminals had long-since replaced the card catalogs of the past. For all that, the library still retained a bit of its mystical intrigue.

"Danny and the Dinosaur," he thought. "That was the first book I ever checked out with my youth library card. I was so proud of that card." As if drawn to retrace the steps of his childhood, he dreamily wandered into the children's books room. The room was splendidly decorated with colorful depictions of famous characters from countless children's books—Dr. Seuss characters, Peter Pan, Winnie the Pooh, and a litany of fairy tale characters. It was a beautiful refuge for young minds. Dating woes and job loss concerns simply drifted away as Mitchell made his way toward the shelves where he expected to find *Danny and the Dinosaur.* He had photocopied a number of pages at five cents a copy, back in the day. Before bed, he would smile as he looked at the pictures of the friendly dinosaur. And there it was! Mitchell carefully pulled the book from the shelf and opened the cover. He was lost in the moment and nearly jumped out of his skin when the librarian addressed him.

"Looking for a book for a friend?"

"Sorry for jumping. You startled me," said Mitchell, trying to recover his composure.

"I should apologize. I didn't mean to sneak up on you like that."

"It's okay. I was just..."

"Doing a research paper on the Dewey Decimal System and your investigations led you here?" kidded the librarian. Mitchell laughed.

"Yes. I was wondering if you might instruct me on some of the finer points of the Dewey Decimal System." Mitchell was rather taken by the young librarian and his blushing cheeks betrayed him. Her face was kind and her beautiful brown eyes were alive and sparkling. The gentle tones of her voice were soothing and reassuring.

"First, perhaps you'd permit me to recommend a book," she said.

"Oh, I think I'll probably be okay with *Danny and the Dinosaur*. It was a childhood favorite. Well, at least in Kindergarten."

"It is an excellent book; I'll give you that. Perhaps you might enjoy this one, too?" The librarian reached over to the shelf and retrieved the book that had been resting adjacent to *Danny and the Dinosaur*. "It's called *Believe in Me, I Said to the Mirror*." She slowly handed the book over to Mitchell, carefully watching his expressions. Mitchell choked as he spoke.

"Danielle Hoff? I'm not familiar with her. Any relation to Syd Hoff, the author of *Danny and the Dinosaur?*"

"Maybe," said the librarian. "It's about a little boy with self-esteem issues. He thinks that no one likes him and he sometimes tries to pretend to be somebody he's not to make friends. But that never works out."

"Whoa. Now don't be giving the ending away. You've sold me on this one, already. But I have one important question."

"Sure. What your question?" asked the librarian, compassion flowing freely from her gentle heart.

"Does it have a happy ending? Because I really need a happy ending right now."

"I think you'll like the ending. In fact, I know you'll love the ending."

"Perfect," said Mitchell, lost in the eyes of the lovely woman standing before him.

"Are you ready for me to check you out?" asked the librarian.

Mitchell thought about seizing the opportunity to make a crude joke about being totally ready to "check her out" but he knew that she deserved better and he knew that he was better than that.

"Yes. Thank you." The two walked over to the counter and the librarian asked for his card. Mitchell realized that he hadn't checked a book out from that library in over ten years and he certainly didn't have an active card. "I'm sorry but I don't have an active card at this library."

"Would you like one?"

"Definitely!" replied Mitchell, enthusiastically. He immediately felt as if he had overplayed his hand and he quickly recomposed himself. "I mean, yes, please."

"My pleasure. If you'll just fill out this paperwork, I can get you a temporary card today and then you should get your permanent card in the mail in the next couple of weeks."

"That'd be great," responded Mitchell, in a calmer tone. His heart rate began to pick up and his palms got sweaty as he considered his next move. "Say, what's your name?" The librarian pointed to her name badge without shifting her eyes from the computer screen where she was entering data to process the temporary card. "Duh. I'm sorry, it's been a hard day. Danielle. That's a pretty name." Mitchell carefully watched Danielle's face for a response but none came. "I'd um, ask you for your number but I left my cell phone in my car. It's had a bad day." Again, Danielle continued with her work but the conversation caught the attention of one of her co-workers who slowly poked her head out from behind one of the shelving units to watch the scene.

"Your books, good sir," said Danielle, with a regal air, as she slid the two books across the counter to Mitchell. Her dismissal of his previous comments had answered Mitchell's questions. Still, he harbored no ill feelings regarding the rejection. Danielle was lovely and a beautiful spirit and he felt at peace in her presence. This visit to the library was time well spent.

"Thank you, milady," Mitchell said, as he bowed. Danielle shot a glance over Mitchell's shoulder, toward the stacks, and her curious co-worker quickly darted out of view. Danielle smiled.

"Have a good day, seeker."

"It's Mitchell, actually."

"I know. I just typed your name into our computer system," Danielle replied with an impish grin.

"Oh, yah, that's right," Mitchell laughed.

"I hope you find what you're looking for," Danielle added, a caring expression coming over her visage.

"Thank you, Danielle. It was a pleasure to meet you."

"Likewise."

"Well, goodbye then," said Mitchell, not wanting the conversation to end and certainly not wanting to close the curtain on the moment. Danielle just nodded and smiled.

Books in hand, Mitchell retraced his steps back to his vehicle and eventually made his way home. The comely librarian had purged his mind of all the dark thoughts that had been piling up throughout the day and, in fact, accumulating over the past few years.

Before retiring for the night, Mitchell sat up in bed, placing the two children's books on his lap as he adjusted the lamp on his nightstand. He read *Danny and the Dinosaur* first and the familiar story brought a smile to his face, once again. "I guess you're never too old for dinosaurs," he thought. The second book, *Believe in Me, I Said to the Mirror,* was something extra special. Mitchell felt silly, crying while reading a child's book, but then he realized that big people and little people all share the same heart and they all seek love and acceptance. The beautiful story was just the medicine Mitchell needed. As he flipped to the last page, a small paper note fell from between the pages to his bed. A name and a phone number were scribbled, in pencil, upon the small piece of white paper. It was from Danielle. Danielle Hoff. Danielle Hoff, the librarian. Danielle Hoff, the author. Danielle Hoff, the woman Mitchell would one day marry and love, unconditionally, for the remainder of his days. She made the world beautiful again. What was lost was found. True love.

TAKING CARE
STELLA ALMAZAN

After 19 years with Ken Dunnston, we were calling it quits.

Ken was the love of my life, my knight in shining armor who rescued me from a doomed first marriage. My first husband, Luke, a primary care internist, was a good man, but our union had been the product of parental urging. The convenience, prestige, and familiarity gleamed like a gem to our elders. I was too young to know any better, liked him fine, and went along with the plan. In only a couple of years, our relationship turned into utter boredom.

Ken grabbed my attention with his Hollywood smile and big personality. I felt in my soul that I'd always wanted someone like Ken, but my confidence as a young woman lacked. His seduction was so smooth and exciting, and I was ready for something new. My self-assurance swelled and I didn't care that I would be foregoing a comfortable life with Luke. While Ken was all glossy on the outside, I saw through to the hardscrabble inside. I was hopelessly smitten by his rough and tumble. My starter husband, Luke, stood in a cloud of dust in my rearview mirror. Thank God we hadn't complicated the break up with any offspring.

Ken and I struggled together in those early years of matrimony, but the toil strengthened our bond. We had only a few dollars at the start, but tons of passion. Ken built a construction business from the ground up. I went from being a nurse to a nurse practitioner. Then I switched gears and became a sales rep for a medical device company. Our hard work paid off and we settled into a well-off, suburban life. We raised handsome, accomplished, twin boys, who were now in college.

Nearly two decades later, marriage felt different. The ambition, the goals, the grind were all missing now. The humdrum and resentment that had crept into my first bout of wedlock now seeped into my second.

Ken, too, had changed. He seemed so taken with me in our honeymoon phase, but the day in and day out of long-term informality had worn us down. We kept in shape for work but rarely put our best foot forward with each other anymore, if ever.

I had seen many middle-aged men turn their heads toward women half their age. I had hoped Ken would be different. But alas, he was not.

With my husband chasing skirts in a full-on mid-life crisis, we parted ways.

"I'll get an apartment." His stoic statement did not come as a surprise. He did not want to be in a home that no longer held meaning for him. "You can have the house."

Even with the foregone conclusion, there was still a certain grief. I dealt with it by jumping headlong into my newfound freedom. I redecorated, took a photography class, went on an African safari, and sailed the fjords of Greenland. It was adventure and peace.

Yet, something was missing. I yearned for someone to share my new life with. Someone whose arm I could grab when the elephant plodded alongside the jeep. Someone to huddle with under an umbrella in the middle of a London downpour. Someone to make love to on a starlit beach in Fiji.

But taking a lover in my early 50s was a daunting proposition. Dating had changed a great deal since the 1980s and 90s. To me, Match.com and Tinder were scary depots of mentally unbalanced mass murderers masquerading as lonely hearts. The lesser evil was to remain contentedly unattached.

———

A late March storm had me shoveling wet, heavy snow from my seemingly endless driveway. I cursed under the clouds of my visible breath about Ken dismissing the idea of installing a heating element.

"Hey, shouldn't Ken be doing that?"

My head snapped up at the car in the street at the end of my drive and the good-natured voice within, chiding me.

"Oh, hi, Steve." I waved and ambled toward his open window. "Whatcha doing in these here parts?"

Steve Cline lived a few streets over in a modest house with an enviable wooded back yard. Our kids were the same age and had played baseball together. He got divorced three years ago when the kids were still in high school. It made the stands a little awkward, especially when he and his ex-wife would bring their current and noticeably younger squeezes.

"I'm returning Wes' chainsaw. Mine broke at the worst time possible. He's got all the tools, that one." He jutted his handsome, stubbled chin in the direction of the enormous yellow house at the end of the cul de sac. Suddenly, I felt self-conscious about my humble abode. It was sturdy brick with ample room and held its own against most other homes in the vicinity, but it was a shack compared to Wes' mansion.

We chatted about Steve's backyard and all the havoc the winter storms wreaked on the trees.

Then he paused and scanned my progress. "How did you get stuck with the shoveling duty? That's not very chivalrous of Ken."

"Oh, well..." I brushed aside my sweaty, dark brown hair poking out from under my woolen winter hat. The massive snowflakes on my lashes weighed on my eyelids as I looked at the rounded toe tips of my Uggs. "...Ken moved out a year ago. The divorce was final in October. You probably didn't hear."

"Oh! No, I didn't."

I could see how he wasn't in the loop. After graduation, the kids sallied forth on their own. There were no more ball games or PTA meetings. Parents lost touch with each other.

I shrugged. "It happens."

"Yeah, I know." He shot me a friendly smirk and a wink. "Any time you want to talk..."

"Thanks." I wasn't sure if he was being cordial or if he really meant it.

"Listen, I'm gonna drop this off at Wes', then I'll be right back and I will finish that for you." He pointed at me playfully. "Don't you touch that shovel! I'll be right back."

"Go on." I tossed my head and waved him off.

Steve raised his window and proceeded cautiously up the snowy street toward my neighbor's. Once his car was a few houses down the road, I resumed my chore.

Each scrape of the shovel brought back memories of Steve as a neighbor and a baseball dad. He worked hard as an anesthesiologist. He cared very much about the town and frequently spoke at township council and school board meetings. Even in the messy divorce days, he was always kind to me and Ken and our twins. He added lively conversation at the parents' table at the end-of-season parties with the team. I never considered him a DILF, but seeing him just now with his scintillating hazel eyes and scruffy, graying, dark blonde hair made me reconsider his appeal.

He's probably seeing somebody. I talked myself out of my delusion. Beads of sweat rolled down my face and stung in the cold breeze as I heaved each swath of snow. I cringed at the unkempt sight of me.

With one more row to go, Steve came back down the street and rolled to a stop.

"Hey, I was going to come back and do that for you!" He called out from the car. "But it looks like you can take care of yourself."

"Thanks for the offer. I would never expect you to do that. What can I say?" I proudly glanced over my shoulder at my accomplishment. "I've handled a lot on my own this year. With some things, though, it's more fun to have someone else do it." I cackled and clunked the shovel against the concrete.

He smiled at my insight and then bit his lip. "Can I...take you to dinner sometime?"

His question knocked the wind out of me, and I leaned on the shovel handle. I wished it could magically hide me looking my worst in a frumpy puffy coat. "O...K...Sure. It would be nice to catch up." I searched his face for an indication -- would this be a friends-date or a date-date? "I thought you might be...you know...with someone."

"Well, I'm not." His smile broadened. "I'll call you."

"I'd like that." I tried to play it cool, even though my insides were doing flips.

We waved to each other as he rode away.

The snowfall had slowed considerably, but the top of the driveway had a thin coat of freshly deposited precipitation. I bounded up to where I had started, and with a few quick passes of the shovel, my work was complete.

———

Two weeks later on a Saturday afternoon, Steve showed up in a blazer and khakis. He had shaved and combed his wavy locks. The hint of musky aftershave hit my nose like a love potion. I had forgotten how charming men could be when they tried.

He took me to a restaurant along the river downtown. I was grateful to escape our prying and gabby enclave. With the wildly fluctuant weather this time of year, it was now mild and pleasant. We took a table outside and watched the city gradually light up as the sun dipped. I drew my moto jacket around me to keep me warm over my tattoo print dress. My outfit was considerably more put together than my snow shoveling duds, but I second-guessed my look. *Were my stiletto boots too much? Was I trying too hard to look hip?* In the back of my mind, conditioned by Ken, I was competing with the 20 and 30-somethings of the world.

The evening sped by with a bottle of pinot and easy conversation. I filled him in on the divorce. He casually mentioned a couple of recent liaisons that didn't work out. We both had been traveling and were captivated by each other's destinations and experiences. The gears in my mind spun. *Could we sojourn together? Could we be a duo?*

Our spirited discussion continued on the way home, but we became nervously quiet as he walked me to the door. On my doorstep, we faced each not knowing what to say, hoping the other would speak first.

"I had a great time." Softly, I broke the awkwardness.

"Me too." He whispered and leaned in to give me a tentative peck that brushed the corner of my mouth. He gauged my reaction. I did not pull away. He planted another kiss squarely and gently on my lips. He tasted of pinot and potential.

"I hope we can do this again." I smiled shyly and blushed at his affection.

"Yes, let's do this again." He kissed me once more, tenderly and fervently, and I melted in his embrace.

———

Sometimes, "let's do this again" is a polite platitude at the end of a date, and I wondered if that might be the case.

I wanted to call Steve so badly, but I didn't want to come across as too eager, or worse, desperate. A couple of days went by with no calls or texts from him. I was puzzled. Especially after such sweet goodnight kisses.

At the 72-hour mark, I couldn't contain myself. I sent a text.

"Hi, Steve."

-- 5 minutes later --

"Hi."

That's it? I was crestfallen.

"I had a really nice time the other night."

"I couldn't get the thought of a trip to Barcelona out of my mind."

Silence.

Flustered at my forwardness, I put the phone on the charger and left it alone.

I was convinced I had made this too easy, and he felt threatened.

Half an hour later, my phone dinged.

"Hey. Sorry. I was in a meeting."

My heart leaped.

"No worries."

"I had a nice time, too."

I didn't reply. I waited for him to add something.

Specifically, I hoped he'd ask me out again. But the screen went dark as I twiddled my thumbs.

At my age, I knew standing by for some desired event never spurred the outcome into fruition, so I took the initiative.

"Would you like to go out again sometime?"

Silence.

Oh, now I've done it.

-- 5 minutes later --

"Yeah, I'd like that."

-- 5 minutes later --

"Sorry. There's a lot going on at work right now."

"I'd like to go out, but maybe in May or June?"

"I'm working weekends for the foreseeable future. I owe my partners for working some weekends for me."

"I want to do this right. I like you. I don't want to be distracted. I have too many balls in the air right now."

I frowned, but also appreciated his candor.

"I understand. I'll get in touch with you May 1. Would that be okay?"

"Yes."

With that, the text exchange ended.

I poured myself a glass of wine and berated myself for catching feelings so quickly. I mindlessly scrolled through social media to displace my angst and frustration.

Among the stream of memes, cat pictures, and political rants, a photo stood out, posted by Russell Parton, a guy I'd met at a friend's party 10 years ago. I probably should have unfollowed or unfriended such a one-time acquaintance, but he only chimed in once in a while, and it was usually something interesting, funny, or insightful.

Two stunning men flanked Russ in his snapshot. The one had shoulders like an Olympian and light brown hair cropped close to his head. The other, in rugged leather style, wore long, flowing, raven-dyed tresses. The three of them, rocking their late 50s like sophisticated college studs, appeared to be in a bar or restaurant for a Boys' Night Out.

I was a bit tipsy and a smidge mad at Steve, and I figured I had nothing to lose.

I messaged him. "Hi, Russ. I don't know if you remember me. I met you at Jerry's party a while back."

I was shocked to immediately see the three dots of a pending reply.

"Of course I do! How are you doing?"

"Good. I like the picture you posted. You guys all look really handsome. Who are your friends? Are they available? Can you introduce me?"

Minutes passed. The waiting game fatigued me. I put the phone down and got ready for bed.

As I slipped under the covers, I checked my phone one last time for the night. Russ had responded.

———

"Sure. They're more business clients than friends, so I'm not certain what their statuses are. But I can make an introduction."

Russ checked with each of the men, and with their permission, shared their contact info. I texted both of them. Texting turned into phone chats. Then I put on my best face as the calls evolved into FaceTime. Despite the progression, something felt off.

"Look, you seem really great. If the timing were different, I'd love to go out with you. But I just started seeing someone." Mr. Shoulders broke the disheartening news through my phone screen. "I have a friend, though, who I think you'd really hit it off with. Rick Chisolm. I'll text you his info."

Mr. Hair Band was next. "You seem like fun. I wish I could meet you in person, but I just got engaged, so I'm off the market. You might want to reach out to my friend, Rick Chisolm. You might really like him."

Their simultaneous suggestion perplexed and intrigued me. Why did both of them string me along? Who was this Rick Chisolm? And why did these two men, who had nothing in common except for a night of shots and darts with a shared consultant, point me toward the same person?

I immediately turned to the world wide web to do some detective work.

Rick was easily searchable and Googlable, yet what he did wasn't exactly clear. All of his profile pictures were magnificent and mysterious. On professional sites, he exuded confidence in a sports coat, coiffed platinum, and barely-there glasses perched precisely with an astute, but approachable, stare behind them. On personal sites, he embodied fitness in athletic attire and favored artistic action shots with his dog.

His radiance and presence were intimidating. I put the idea of him out of my mind.

I messaged Russ again. "Thanks for connecting me with your business associates. They seem like great guys, but they're both spoken for."

"Well, that's too bad."

A moment later, he added a sheepish post-script. "You know, I'm available."

My heart stopped in embarrassment. I clicked on his profile to see if I missed a change of status update. He didn't have one listed. "Oh, Russ. I didn't know." My mind raced, grasping for distant details. "Didn't I also meet your wife at Jerry's party? Dolores, right?"

"Yes."

Yes, wife? Not ex-wife? Whoa. What's this? He's married, but available? My heart thumped at this unexpected and confusing twist.

"She died a couple of years ago. Breast cancer."

My heart dropped. I went back to his profile and swiped through his photos. He had nothing recent of him and Dolores together. Again I glanced at the photograph that had caught my attention, the trio of men. Russ, in the middle, was shorter than the other two, but had his own unique attributes with thick, salt and pepper hair and black-framed glasses. He smiled slightly for the camera, but there was an underlying sadness in his eyes that I hadn't noticed before.

"Oh my. I was not aware. I'm so sorry. I feel awful for missing this news. My deepest sympathies."

"Thank you. I didn't post about it. Actually, I left social media for a while. It was really tough."

I felt like a heel for my ignorance. I wanted to say something compassionate but came up empty. My feeble attempt manifested as a crass blurt. "Wanna grab coffee sometime?"

"Yes. That would be wonderful."

I sensed him smiling through his message. My heart found itself back in place.

———

Russ and I met at the Cake and Biscuit. The bakery was tucked into the nook of a tree-lined strip of village boutiques. We sat at a cafe table in the front courtyard. The spring afternoon sun filtered through the serenely stirring buds and branches overhead.

We sipped on our coffees and the conversation flowed as if we were at our own personal party for two. The trace of melancholy had lifted, replaced with happy crinkles in the corners of Russ' eyes when he laughed. Two hours had passed like two minutes.

Out of the blue, an ingenue in a smart dress and sneakers approached our table and startled us.

"Dad?"

"Vida! Sweetheart!" Russ jumped up and kissed his daughter on the cheek. "What a surprise to see you. What are you doing here?"

"I'm picking up cupcakes for the boss' kid's birthday party." She turned her head to her father, then to me, then back to her father.

"Vida, this is Ms. Dunnston."

We shook hands.

"Very nice to meet you."

I felt her eyes inspecting me. We made small talk about work and the nice weather as Russ took his seat across from me again and watched our repartee. She gave me another covert scan before heading into the shop.

"Russ, she's beautiful and poised and so industrious and observant." I reached over and touched his arm. "You must be so proud."

"She takes after her mother." He winced fondly toward the bakery and then down to his nearly empty coffee cup. A touch of blue reappeared in his brown eyes.

Vida emerged from the store with several large boxes of baked goods.

"Really nice meeting you." She tilted her head to me with a warm smile.

I rejoined the friendly farewell.

Russ got up to help her with the car door. I caught her giving her dad a surreptitious nod before dashing off.

———

I liked Russ, and I hoped he liked me, too. As with Steve, I waited a few days before calling.

When he answered, he slurred. "Coffee wiz you zaother day was awezome."

I checked my watch. It was 12:30. *Had he been drinking?*

"I loved it, too. Is everything okay, Russ?"

"Yeah. Fantastic. What could be bether zan mimozas and brunch? Well, mostly mimozas." He wavered. "Actually, no, I'm not really fantastic."

I sank into my couch and listened to his intoxicated jabber.

"You...you...are terrific. And I thought we might...but I can't. Seeing Vida...and then Dolores...I'm not...I'm not..."

"You're not ready to move on yet?" I felt misled by him piping up about being single and ready to mingle, but I also believed he had genuinely wanted to give it a try.

"Right! Right! I'm sorry. I thought I was, but I'm not." He started to cry. "I'm afraid I'm never going to get over Dolores."

"Russ," I tried to allay his remorse, "a part of you will never be over her, and it's okay. And it's okay to need more time." I let out a sympathetic sigh. "Are you getting help? It sounds like you might need someone to help you get through this. Like, someone professional."

"Yes. Vida is making some calls." He perked up as he spoke her name. "She really enjoyed meeting you the other day."

"I liked meeting her, too." Thinking back to the delightful afternoon at the Cake and Biscuit brought a smile to my face. "I'd be happy to have coffee with you again sometime. I'll wait to hear from you, though. Whenever you think the time is right. But please, take care of yourself."

"Thank you. Thank you. I'm sorry. Again. I'm so sorry."

We hung up, and my heart ached from being tugged in so many directions. The pain impaired my judgment, and I texted Steve.

"Hi."

"Hi."

"I know it's not quite May yet, but do you want to get lunch sometime?"

"It doesn't have to be a weekend."

"I'd love to, but things are still really crazy."

"I promise, the minute it settles down, I'll call you."

Shot down again, I wallowed in self-doubt.

I scrolled through my recent text messages. I stopped when I got to the back-and-forths with Mr. Shoulders and Mr. Hair Band. I still had another card to play: Rick Chisholm.

———

It took me a couple of weeks to get up the courage to send a "hello" text, but Rick was surprisingly down to earth. After some initial bandying, Rick proposed a FaceTime chat.

Seeing him in motion on my screen was even more mesmerizing than the still photos of him on the web. His smooth voice spilled from his mouth like molten butterscotch and his icy blue eyes glistened like diamonds. With gentlemanly courtesy, he deferred to me in our discourse and spoke minimally about himself. Even with our effortless video chat, he remained an enigma. The shroud around him drew me in and I wanted to know more.

"I'd like to take you out." His words reverberated as a benevolent imperative, not a request. "A friend of mine is having a party. I'd like for you to be my guest."

What an interesting first date. "What kind of party is it?"

"Very exclusive. He has these get-togethers about four times a year. For certain movers and shakers."

I was flattered he considered me for this occasion. "What should I wear?"

"Something like this." He tilted his camera down to show his designer suit enveloping his hale male figure. Despite having every reason to brag, he came across as unpretentious and generous. "I know people at this party will be dressed for success, but not with anything too fussy or fancy with a lot of jewelry or decorative buttons or ornate clasps. I'm happy to have a dress sent over."

I was taken aback. *Money must be no object for this guy.* A new outfit tempted me, but to avoid the strings that came with gifts, I declined. "Thank you. I should have something along those lines."

"Superb. I'll see you Saturday, then."

———

In the process of getting ready, my bedroom looked ransacked, with clothes strewn everywhere. Finally, I settled on one of ten little black dresses in my closet, after rejecting the red and violet and blue ones. The body contoured trappings hit above the knee and featured a single front zipper along the midline with a generous hoop fob to enhance the slider.

"Nice, but not too fussy." I gave a satisfied nod to my reflection in the mirror and put on my power hoop earrings to match.

Though I had protested, Rick insisted on sending me a breath-taking pair of Louboutins, supplemented with a dozen roses and a card: "Looking forward to an exhilarating evening."

I had just fluffed my salon-primed hair and applied the last swipe of deep-red lipstick when Rick arrived at precisely 8:00.

When I opened the door, he greeted me with all the earnestness of a prom date but carried himself with the savvy of a CEO. He wore his tailored suit with no tie and the shirt unbuttoned just enough to show a hint of attentively manscaped chest.

His appreciative stare lingered. My suave suitor took my hand and kissed it. "You look...exquisite."

"Thank you. And thank you for the roses. And the shoes." I pointed my toe to model the luxurious high heels, which accentuated my toned muscles. I felt like Cinderella.

"They look lovely on you." He grinned like Prince Charming. "Shall we?"

He offered his arm and escorted me down the driveway to the

waiting stretch limousine. I imagined Wes snooping from the bay window of his looming yellow castle at the end of the street. *Eat your heart out, Wes.*

The driver came around to open the door.

"Thank you, Oliver." He nodded at the chauffeur.

With Rick's hand on the small of my back, he stretched his other arm toward the ritzy portal. "After you."

Upon entering the spacious cabin, I momentarily froze at the sight of two gorgeous ladies already inside. One had a long, straight, blonde bob; the other, the exact same hairstyle, but in auburn. I suspected they were in their 40s, but with their lithe physiques and impeccable makeup, they could have passed for 30.

Rick made introductions and referred to them as "his friends who were joining us for the party." He swiveled into place at the end of the long seat next to the ice bucket. "Champagne, ladies?"

He passed the flutes of Dom Perignon all around, and we toasted and sipped. Soon I had an agreeable buzz going. I noticed there was plenty of room, but the other two women had scooched to either side of me, unconventionally close.

"You're so pretty." Babette, the blonde, cooed, as she leaned forward to tuck a wisp of my wavy, chestnut curls behind my ear. Beneath her black fringe flapper dress, held up by spaghetti straps, her abounding bosom swayed as she moved. Her short hem rode up and her crossed legs brushed mine every so often as we rounded the tight turns of our wooded route.

"You're both very beautiful." I turned to Babette, then to Rebecca, whose tie-sashed, black kimono evening gown highlighted her ravishing décolletage.

"You have a great body. What's your secret?" Rebecca put her delicate hand on my knee. "Do you work out?"

"I try to take care of myself." An unexpected tingling shot through me as my gaze met Rebecca's, as intense and smoldering as a model's.

Starved for any type of courtship, I found the overtures from

Rebecca and Babette strangely titillating. I couldn't discern whether the champagne had brought out a warm welcome from their inner sorority girl or whether they were coming on to me. I had never been into women, but these two exuded irresistible allure.

My eyes darted to Rick, semi-reclined, swilling his bubbly with smug relaxation. I couldn't help but notice the unmistakable bulge in his fitted trousers. For a man of contemporaneous age, I was glad of his function, and also, bewildered.

"A little something for the soiree," Babette murmured in my ear as she slipped a small coin purse into my velvet clutch.

The way things were going, I figured it contained either weed or speed, but my heady surroundings made me quickly forget about Babette's largesse. My three companions leered at me in a pleased and dreamy way. With all the champagne coursing through my brain, I didn't mind.

For an instant, I let my mellow inebriation betray my curiosity. "So what kind of party is ---"

"Mr. Chisholm, Ladies, we have arrived." Oliver's respectful baritone with a faux British accent interrupted my inquiry as the limo pulled up to a well-lit, neomodern estate of stone and glass in a clearing in the forest.

Oliver attended to the door, and the four of us climbed out. Rick offered me his arm again, which I appreciated. Champagne and opulent spike heels were not an orthopedically sound combination. Plus, it reinforced to me that I was his date, and the other two were simply along for the ride. The entire scenario was electric and bizarre, but the sparkling spirits nudged me into feeling recklessly bold for whatever the wild night held in store.

Babette and Rebecca addressed the bouncer at the front door with a kiss on each cheek, then proceeded inside.

But the guard with his thick legs akimbo and his muscly arms crossed stopped me and Rick. He bowed graciously to me with a gallant smile, "Good evening, madame." Then he faced Rick and motioned him inside. "Mr. Chisholm. A word, please?"

Rick adjusted his cufflinks and cocked his swagger. "I'll be right back."

They disappeared behind the thick oak door with resplendent knockers. I tried to see what was happening through the windows, but all I could make out were shadows, music, and revelers' laughter. Suddenly, I remembered Babette's provision and wondered if that had aroused security's suspicions.

I dug into my clutch and opened the pouch to see what illegal offering she had transferred to me. Inside I discovered a stash of unequivocally legal condoms. The blood drained from my face and I gasped. *This is a fucking orgy!*

My hands shook as I stuffed the ribald sachet back into hiding. My mind swam with Rick's mention of "movers and shakers" and his point about complicated clothing being passé. My instincts told me to run, but in every direction, the pitch-black swallowed the terra incognita. Plus, fleeing under the influence with 5-inch pins on my heels would be inviting disaster.

As the minutes ticked by while I waited for Rick, my thoughts settled. I contemplated my predicament with more composure and recognized I was a reasonably put-together middle-aged woman, accompanied by a chimerically hot man, packing protection, about to partake in clandestine cocktails. I had never been to a sex party, and this could be my only chance.

Rick reappeared without the doorman. His face was flushed, and yet, he appeared calm and collected.

"Listen, the hostess is limiting the party to previous guests only. She is a friend and expects me inside, but unfortunately, without you. I do appreciate you coming all this way. I was looking forward to getting to know you better." His eyes imperceptibly dipped toward my pumps. "Surely another time. I'll have Oliver bring you home."

A mixture of relief and letdown churned inside me. "Really, it's fine, Rick. The limo ride was actually kind of fun." I glanced down at my well-heeled toes and thought about the strings. "About the shoes..."

"They're yours. Please enjoy them. I'd like to see you again in them. " He escorted me to the car as Oliver pulled into the drive, and with a double cheek kiss, bid me adieu. "Oliver, please take care of our splendid guest."

"Yes, sir, Mr. Chisholm."

As the limo coursed back through the woods over hill and dale, I thought about everything leading up to this fateful night. Why did Rick think I might enjoy such unrestrained indulgence? Was it an insult or a compliment? Did Mr. Shoulders and Mr. Hairband know this was Rick's game? Had they been to one of these parties? Did I come across as only a randy divorcee looking for a hookup? Who was the hostess? How could she wield even more power than Rick, as if that were possible? And why was she being so uber-exclusive? Did she think I was undercover law enforcement or the media? So many unanswerable questions swirled in my spinning head.

"My good lady, if I may..." Oliver politely engaged with me via the rearview mirror. "Some proprietors are extremely particular. I wouldn't take it personally."

"What happens in there?" I shifted in my seat, thinking about whether Rick might have the benefit of Rebecca or Babette right now, or both. "Have you ever been inside?"

"No, ma'am. I wouldn't know firsthand." His eyes returned to the curvy road. "But I would say, guests come away rather...satisfied."

We pulled up in front of my house, and Oliver ushered me to the front door. I gave him a grateful smile and studied his kind face. For a moment, I pondered what Rick meant by Oliver taking care of me.

"Oliver, would you like to come -- "

"I must return to the festivities. My duty to Mr. Chisholm calls. It has been a pleasure." He bent forward and with a gloved hand tipped his chauffeur's cap. "Have a glorious evening, my good lady."

My face pinked at his professionalism.

He waited until I was safely inside before returning to the driver's seat. I watched the polished, elongated vehicle disappear into the darkness.

For the first time in hours, I didn't feel like a specimen under the microscope. I kicked off my heels and muttered. "There's no place like home."

I immediately ran upstairs, unzipped my dress, and slithered out. I washed off the layers of frippery. Then, with the scattered contents of my closet still blanketing my bed like old friends expecting my homecoming, I crawled between the sheets.

With an exhausted brain and body, I fell asleep as soon as my head hit the pillow. But even in slumber, I couldn't escape my torment.

I dreamed of being completely exposed on an unfamiliar couch in an unfamiliar house with Rick deftly plundering any opportunity I presented to him. Oddly, aside from his grip on the scarlet soles of my high-end kicks, I didn't feel anything, as if he were only a mirage. Behind him were distorted versions of Mr. Shoulders and Mr. Hair Band and Russ and Steve, all waiting their turn. Meanwhile, Babette and Rebecca, wearing nothing but black thongs and Loubs, circled the spectacle with their cell phones taking photos and video.

My dream conspired with a hot flash, and I woke in a puddle of sweat. Instinctively, my hand drifted to the cleft between my legs. I rolled over to rummage through my nightstand. I lubed up my magic wand and took care of my pent-up need as the first glimmer of dawn glowed through my closed blinds.

My tension subsided with every blissful spasm. In the wake of my frenzy, a wave of clarity washed over me: men weren't worth the trouble. Perhaps I was only looking to get my groove back. However, going solo was just fine.

———

Late May enlivened my typically empty house with a whirlwind of activity. The twins were home from college, and yet, never home, as they rushed in and out from visits with their father, their summer jobs, and carousing with friends.

In the quiet moments, I planned my year of travel. Alone. This included a last-minute trip to Fiji in early June. *It will be good to get away. Far away.*

One evening, the boys announced they were meeting up with some buddies from their old baseball team. This reminded me that May 1st had come and gone, and I hadn't contacted Steve as I said I would. I shook off the thought. It didn't matter much anymore.

My excitement mounted as I counted down the days to my trip. I packed my bags and brought them down to the foyer the evening before my flight. As I delivered my carry-on to the growing constellation of travel paraphernalia, I heard my phone rattling on the kitchen counter.

I rushed over and drew my head back at the caller id.

"Steve?"

"Hi."

"What a surprise. It's been a while."

"Yeah." His voice was low and contrite like he wanted to make amends. "You know, it's a nice night. Too nice to enjoy alone. Would you like to come over? I'll make a fire. We can just hang out."

I hesitated and stifled a sigh. Indeed, it was the beginning of a perfect early summer night. The cloudless day was dissolving into sunset, which would deepen into a cool, crystal clear twilight. I had no grand designs on my evening other than rifling through my maps and brochures for the umpteenth time. My bags were packed, and lounging by the fire on such a picturesque night sounded like a decent way to wind down. "Okay. But I can't stay long. I have plans in the morning."

"Do you want me to pick you up?" He did his best to temper his excitement.

"No, no. I'll drive over. It's no problem." I didn't want to be stuck at Steve's until the wee hours.

"Ok." He covered up his disappointment, but I could hear him grinning. "See you in a bit."

When I got there, I padded around to the back patio. Stacks of firewood, remnants of the winter's fallen trees, bordered the back-yard. I found him crouched at the fire pit, poking the logs with a stick.

He glanced up at me, taking it all in, from my Chucks to my ripped jeans and t-shirt, topped with a plaid flannel shirt. The gentle breeze fanned the fire which cast a glow on his keen face. His eyes widened as he beheld the casual me, just as Rick's had with me all done up. "You look...great."

I tilted my head with a tentative smile.

"I'm sorry I haven't been available." He stared into the flames. "I've never been any good at multitasking or compartmentalizing or whatever it's called these days. Maybe that's why I haven't been able to make it work with anyone."

His psychobabble bored me. I had no interest in bolstering his self-pity. "It's neither here nor there, Steve." I waved my arm at the vast outdoor expanse. "It's a fabulous night. Let's just enjoy it."

"Of course." He broke from his flame-induced hypnosis and poured two glasses of pinot. We clinked. "To June."

Steve had thrown some blankets on the adirondak chairs. The fire warmed us as we sank back into the cozy seats, sipped our drinks, and surveyed the emerging stars against the darkening celestial backdrop.

Steve, lost in overwhelming space, finally spoke. "Have you ever been to Fiji?"

"No." A bright, moving dot in the heavens caught my eye. I made a silent wish on the shooting star. As I fixed on it, though, I realized it was only the glow of an airplane, bisecting the infinite black between the brilliant points of light. "But it's high on my list."

AN OBTAINABLE ILLUSION

LUISA REYES

Cathleen stared at Ginger Rogers' long flowing dress in the classic movie dance sequence on the television screen longingly. She couldn't remember the last time she had the opportunity to dress up in such elegant attire and attend a truly gracious function. For nowadays it seemed like the default attire of a faded T-shirt and worn-looking blue jeans were widely considered appropriate for most anything except perhaps a heavily made-up female news anchor on an ultra-conservative right-wing news network. And their attire was a far cry from the sophistication of Ginger Rogers' long dresses swirling about as she smoothly flows along on the ballroom dance floor, to say the least.

Cathleen let out a long sigh. She had heard stories from her grandparents growing up about how during the Great Depression they were considered fortunate to have something in their sandwiches at school besides lard. So, she knew that the refinement perpetuated in the late 1930s era classic movie she was watching had a bit of the illusory element to it even during the time of its initial release. But, oh! It was such an appealing illusion. Yet, the words he had said the day before kept repeating themselves in her mind. "You have personality, but . . ."

There was no mistaking to what he was alluding to in his unfinished sentence. As his attractive assistant walked up and reached for his arm possessively, it immediately became clear that he had chosen passion over personality. And as the scene replayed itself in Cathleen's mind, she recalled how even the look of his eyes had transitioned from bearing the kindly glint to which she was accustomed to reflecting a dark, almost malicious look. It had all been so surreal.

She shrugged her shoulders. It wasn't the first time Cathleen had lost a guy due to her traditional values and it likely wouldn't be the last. But with the passing of time, she was beginning to feel more and more alone with the ways of the world. Which were oddly becoming the ways of the sacred as well as the secular. Cathleen could bear it no longer. She turned off the movie and decided to retire to bed early. After all, she had promised her friend that she would help her promote the upcoming race for breast cancer awareness at the tailgating on the quadrangle tomorrow. An event that would involve a lot of walking and it was best to be well-rested for what was likely to be a long and busy day.

Although Cathleen arrived early the next morning to where the large southern university's home football game festivities were taking place; the pop music was already blasting loudly, the beer was already flowing freely and parking spaces were already hard to find. Especially ones that weren't being rented for the day at a pricey premium. It all seemed so decidedly *common* to Cathleen. Especially since the only song she was really in the frame of mind to hear was Mimi's "Donde Lieta" aria from the opera "La Boheme".

When she had first learned the classic aria she thought Mimi was exaggeratedly kind. But now she could relate to the words of "Addio, senza rancor" so well. After all, goodbye without bitterness was how she had felt that evening when he praised her personality so highly . . . only to choose something else.

Finding a free parking spot far away, but not too distant from the football game hoopla, Cathleen seized the opportunity to park. Giving her long flowing hair a brush through and then texting her friend that she had arrived and would be at the center of the quadrangle as soon as her feet would take her.

While Cathleen disdained it all as bordering on the boorish, the excitement filling the air was a bit contagious even so. And she felt her spirits rise as she walked past several people all decked out in their home team attire. Giving her a "high five" with their hands as they let out a loud cheer for the home team. Making a smile radiate on Cathleen's face.

Meandering farther along, she soon reached the street leading to the quadrangle that was lined with restaurants doubling as bars that neighbored the main drag of the university. The crowds were massive that day and the fraternity boys and sorority girls were filling every available nook and corner on the sidewalks that were left available. Before long, Cathleen was approached by a pair of fraternity brothers who were a bit tipsy with the words of, "Please fuck me." Cathleen merely rolled her eyes as she figured out how to walk past them and their inebriated state.

Another block down and Cathleen was tapped on the back by another pair of soused fraternity boys. Turning around out of habit, she was promptly met with, "My roommate here thinks you're cute. Won't you fuck his face off?"

"I'll let you do it for me," she responded and hurriedly set some distance between them as much as the massive crowd of people would permit.

Knowing that she was often mistaken for looking younger, Cathleen was still finding it hard to believe these fraternity boys were taking her for being literally half her age. Of course, the effects of the alcohol blurring their senses must be helping, she concluded. But, when she had agreed to help her friend, she had thought she was long past the notice of these too-moneyed for their own good types.

"What's up, babe? Wanna fuck?" were the next words to defile her ears from a fraternity boy who wouldn't be unpalatable were he not on the verge of becoming plastered before the chimes on the quadrangle struck the noon hour. Cathleen shook her head in the negative with a feeling of relief coming over her as the movement of the crowd naturally pushed him away from her.

"My goodness! Do these vulgar come-ons actually work for them?" Cathleen found herself wondering as she continued along her way. For she couldn't think of anything less appealing than the ways of these frat boys and their ridiculous Oedipus complexes. However, as she glanced at a trio of sorority girls dressed in something akin to a mini skirt dress and shorts outfit where the hemlines and the neck-lines both converged in the middle underneath their belly buttons, she was beginning to think that maybe these boys and their crude idioms weren't entirely unwelcome in some circles.

Approaching by now the fraternity houses that were across from the football stadium, Cathleen with her dark brown eyes took notice of how they were enjoying the sunny day by listening to some live rock bands in their front lawns. With some of them playing beer pong and one group even throwing some footballs back and forth. When yet another set of male voices approached her with their four-letter word introductions Cathleen side stepped them as best as she could.

"How glad I am that I didn't go here for undergrad" Cathleen thought to herself. For she was already feeling weary of having to continually find ways of ignoring these befuddled boys and the day was far from being over. For a moment she found herself wishing she were back at home safely watching her classic movie. Yet, *"it is all an illusion,"* she told herself.

Completely, lost in her contemplations, all of a sudden a whizzing sound manifested itself in her ears. And in the in-between state of being lost in her thoughts and becoming aware of her surroundings, Cathleen was dumbfounded to see a big giant football that had been overthrown from one of the fraternity houses come barreling right towards her. She had heard of people being killed by something even so flimsy as a folded-over paper airplane hitting the temples of their heads. But, never had she dreamed she would meet her demise in such a way when "Whack!"

A big arm from behind her reached over and knocked the football out her way. Sparing Cathleen from such a premature end. Breathing a heavy sigh of relief and gratitude. The tall young man who had freed her from the football's impending forceful hit was now standing by her side. And Cathleen thanked him as she became fully aware of what had happened.

"You're a hero!" the young ladies walking behind them said. And they soon insisted that Cathleen must have her picture taken with him. As they moved to the side of the mass throng of people heading towards the quadrangle, they posed for their picture. And the tall rescuer expressed his honor at having merely been there to do the right thing at the right time.

"You must exchange phone numbers!" The young ladies continued in their light-hearted glee, a bit to Cathleen's embarrassment. But, she nonetheless acquiesced. And after they parted ways, she realized what she would be doing once she got back home that evening. For she no longer felt it was an unobtainable illusion. She would turn on her classic movie and thoroughly enjoy it from beginning to end.

NOSTALGIA
NATALIE CARROLL

"Gravitation cannot be held responsible for people falling in love. How on earth can you explain in terms of chemistry and physics so important a biological phenomenon as first love? Put your hand on a stove for a minute and it seems like an hour. Sit with that special person for an hour and it seems like a minute. That's relativity."- Albert Einstein

Wrapped in the cocoon that was my duvet, nice, warm, and cozy surrounded by darkness, life was good. That was until my curtains were abruptly opened by my mum. Blinded by the beam from the sun my vision hazy as I adjust to the landing of living. Urgh, morning, the worst part of the day for any teenager. Sadly it was the beginning of another slow week. With that, I dragged myself out of bed moaning and groaning as I mumbled under my breath about how I didn't want to go to school.

"Hurry up, you're going to be late!" fog-horned my mum.

. . .

Reluctantly, I got dressed, packed my bag and rushed downstairs. Mum had made my breakfast but after spending those extra twenty minutes in my bed, I didn't have time for breakfast. I swiped up a slice of toast and a sip of orange juice and out the door I went.

As I had arrived the bell had just went. And still, I hadn't attained all the books out of my locker. Rushing down what seemed to be the long and endless corridor. Quickly I swiped up my books and made my way to class. However, it was those few minutes that changed my life...

I quickly made my way up the stairs and almost made it to my class or at least I thought I did before I bumped into him.

"Hey, sorry about that." A soft voice said.

"It's fine..." I said with a hushed whispered voice.

I look up to him with his hair, dark and lustrous, with a sheen like fine hardwood. But that comparison isn't entirely fair, I suppose. Hardwood doesn't swish gently like his hair does, swaying with the words he spoke. A shiny varnish catches merely light around it, but the depths of that deep chestnut brown reflected all the radiance of his smile. But it was his soft brown eyes that poured into my own pools of dark brown. I suddenly found myself reaching just beneath his chin as he stood at full height. His eyes locked onto mine, I couldn't help but blush a little as he looked into my eyes. It was just then that I felt my heart melt as I found myself lost under his seizing hypnotic spell.

As we stood there gazing at one another. I felt as though I seemed to have seen everything I had ever needed to see just from looking into his eyes. Perhaps, maybe time itself had frozen in those short few minutes we spent in one another's company. As much as I was enjoying the escape of being in another world, I suddenly found myself being reintroduced to reality. I noticed the clock on the wall by the corner of my eye.

. . .

"Oh no, I'm late! I'm sorry but I've got to go!" I said as I ascended into a state of panic.

As I fled the scene he shouted,

"Wait! Where are you going? I didn't even get your name."

I glanced back at him and gave him a smile as I quickly made my way down the corridor like a racecar. I finally arrived at my class, I opened the door and stepped into the classroom - all eyes were on me as the centre of attention, which is something that I don't like being.

"Ah miss Bloom, I see you've finally decided to greet us with your presence. Please by all means tell us what has kept you from joining us for so long," Mrs. Roglort said sarcastically.

Embarrassed, my face lights up like a red traffic light, "Nothing, Miss.... I just had a late start to the day, sorry," I quietly said.

"Well, in that case, could you make sure it doesn't happen again?" Mrs. Roglort said as she looked down at me through her glasses.

After Mrs. Roglort had finished talking, I rushed to the back of the classroom to my seat and buried my head in what can only be described as embarrassment into the next century.

As time went on I couldn't help but think about the guy I had ran into. I hadn't seen him around school since our introduction. Come to think of it, I have never seen him around school. He was pretty cute too. And yet I became so infatuated to know who he was. I found myself browsing through my Facebook feed - as I do, and then I noticed that I had a friend request. It was him!

Thoughts ran like Usain Bolt in the 2008 Olympics through my mind. I couldn't help but think to myself: Why would he want to add me? Wait, how does he know who I am? What do I say if he wants to talk to me? Should I accept it? Oh, what should I do!? After squabbling with myself, contemplating what I should do I decided to force myself to press that button. It was from there where it all began, where that one message changed everything.

"Hey Delilah 🖤" He typed.

Gazing at the screen in riddles as I tried to think what to reply back. My stomach filled with butterflies, as my fingertips anxiously hovered and twitched over the keyboard.

Oh my god, I can't believe he knows I exist! Oh my god, he put a heart after my name! What should I reply back?

After calming down a bit I finally got the courage to type, "Hey x."

"How have you been?" He replied.

"Yeah, I'm good, thanks. Yourself?" I replied back.

"Yeah, I'm good," He replied.

It wasn't long before the conversation ran dryer than the Sahara desert, as we ran out of things to say to each other. Meanwhile, my thoughts were like a run-away train skimming through my mind.

"Christopher," I hesitated to type the rest of the sentence "can I ask you something?"

"Sure." He replied.

"Why are you speaking to me?" I nervously typed, scared to know the answer.

"Well... last time if you remember I didn't get a chance to speak to you after you ran away from me like Cinderella. But I've seen you around school and I think you're cool. And quite frankly I think you're cute :p"

He thinks I'm cute!

"Awww you're sweet 🖤" I replied.

"Besides I know you can't resist my devilish handsome looks :p" he typed with a cheeky face emoji.

Rolling my eyes as I read his last message, I couldn't help but smile a little, as I knew the truth of how I felt. Maybe it was love at first sight, or perhaps I was falling for his devilish, boyish charms that made me fall weak at the knees.

"Let me guess you have that effect on all girls, they just become so swoon by the mysterious persona you project," I replied.

"Not all girls... just most of them, but let me guess you're not like the average girl that attends our school? " he typed back.

"And what kind of girl would you class me as then?" I asked.

"Someone who is above average anyway, wonderful springs to mind really for me," he replied.

I smiled and rolled my eyes as I read his message knowing it was only a line he was using "Again does that line work on all the girls?"

"I could quote Shakespeare if you would prefer my dear, but I suppose you'll have to wait till next time when we talk. Bye for now kid :p"

And like that, before I could even say goodbye, he was offline.

I spent the rest of that night thinking of our conversation. I couldn't believe he thought that I was cute! The couple of hours we spent talking only felt like a few minutes. I fell asleep that night with a smile that I never knew I had.

It was the next morning, as I went about doing my usual daily routine. Before I knew it I was back home. As I was getting on with my homework, I found myself browsing through my Facebook as I do. Looking through my newsfeed and one thing led to another and I found myself looking through his profile.

I know what you're thinking but I don't always go on his profile and basically stalk him... okay maybe I do a little, but is that such a bad thing?

A few days have passed since we last spoke. It seemed like forever. It was as if I had a compulsory addiction. Just to talk with him for a little bit longer, would have been enough for this withdrawal. Every chance I would get I would check if he was online. Hoping he would pop up. Every time I would receive a message or a notification, I would hope it would be from him.

It was the day after and my withdrawal wasn't as bad, I was okay and coping - as far as I was concerned. Several tests to look forward to were on my agenda. And as usual I was late for class, but none of that mattered when I found myself in his presence.

"You know we need to stop meeting like this," he said with his arms crossed as he leaned against my locker. "Unless you're stalking me? Are you? I think you're definitely stalking me. There's nothing wrong with that of course, I mean you're a cute stalker." He said as he smirked a little.

I suddenly found myself lost under those soft brown eyes, as I smiled like an idiot.

"So since by the looks of things you haven't made it to class, why don't we ditch school for the day and go do something fun?"

"I can't do that!? I'll get caught, we both will!" I protested.

At that moment he held his hand out, "Trust me, we won't." he said as he smiled.

I began to reach my hand out but became hesitant. I paused.

"Please, for me, come with me?" he said, as he gave me the puppy-eyed look.

How could I say no to those puppy eyes? Without giving any consideration I placed my hand in his and off we went running through the corridor and out the doors.

After a while we had gotten away from school we ended up taking a stroll down to a small stream. And our hands were still locked into each other. The small river was surrounded by a summer's lush green grass, whilst the wind blew a gentle breeze. We soaked in the rays from the sun's light.

"So what do you think?" asked Christopher.

"It's beautiful. I've never seen something so beautiful," I said, amazed at the view.

"Neither have I," he mumbled as he glanced in my direction. "I'm going to dip my feet in if you want to join," Christopher said.

"I think I'll just sit here," I said.

I sat at the side and watched as he dipped his feet in the river. I should have seen what happened next.

"Hey, Delilah?" he said.

"Yeah?" I said with hesitation.

A cold shower of water comes over me.

As I froze from the shock of the coldness, all that left me was a high-pitched squeak.

"You looked a bit too hot, I thought I would cool you down," he said, shrugging his shoulders and smirking with that gorgeous smile of his.

"You did not just do that!?" I said, shocked.

He splashed me again.

"I believe I did now." He said with that goofy look on his face that he gave me.

I paused for a moment before I made my way towards him to get my revenge, only to embarrassingly fall on my back in the river.

"Are you okay? I'll help you up," he said concerned as he held his hand out.

I reached out to grab his hand, only to pull him down with me. He falls into the river lying next to me. We both laughed it off. He gave me that quirky smile that I had loved since the first day I had met him. He stands up holding his hand out for me to take. I grab his hand and suddenly I find myself in the first position all over again. Our body's close, my head just under his chin I couldn't stop my heart from setting off ticking like a bomb inside my chest. My blood rapidly flowing into my rosé cheeks, my face became red as ever. Our heads drew together like magnets. He caressed my supple cheek; he lifted my chin; our noses almost touching. He leaned in; close I could smell the minty flavour coming from his breath as it brushed the top of my lip. My hand placed firmly on his muscular chest, as I gently grabbed his shirt. His lips reached my jaw, tracing the lines of my ear to my collarbone. They were so warm against my ruby red lip-gloss. I felt a romantic wave rushing to my heart as his lips danced across mine. They reminded me of soft fluffy pillows. Lifting my hands from his chest I pulled them up high to his shoulders, where I entwined them with his soft dark brown hair. It was here where I found myself wrapped up in him, body, heart and soul. As I was falling head over heels for Christopher.

He pulled away, only to look into my eyes as he put a strand of my hair behind my ear. It was from that moment, I never knew it was possible to fall for someone like how I fell for him.

Strolling down the street as we held hands...

"Delilah?" Christopher nervously asked.

"Yeah?" I curiously said.

Whatever he had to say to me he was hesitating.

"Okay..." he exhales. "The... the thing is..." he bites the bullet, "I've liked you for three years, and as the years have passed by I've fallen for you. I love you. More and more as the days pass us by. I know, that's probably a strong word to say but there's no other word that describes how I truly feel about you."

My heart stopped... I was left speechless. I've been waiting for this since the day we met and now I'm hesitant. I mean I like him too but... but would it work out between us?

"Say something please?" begged Christopher.

"I will admit I like you too, but I mean I'm a nobody in school and well you... you're popular. We live in two separate worlds; I don't think I could deal with the judgments of others," I said.

"You know what I think? I say who cares what others think. If you're happy and I'm happy we should take a chance," said Christopher.

Christopher and I had been together for a couple of weeks and it was going great. It was a usual lazy weekend for me as I curled up watching a bit of TV, when suddenly the doorbell rang - it was Christopher.

"Yes, can I help you?" I jokingly said.

"Hey stranger," he said as he leaned against the wall crossing his arms. "I would have called but then I wouldn't have got to see the expression on your face when I turned up unannounced," he said.

"You do realise I look like a scruff right? You couldn't have come at a better time." I said.

"I'm glad you think so because I couldn't have come at a time when you looked anymore beautiful," said Christopher.

From a distance, my mother's voice was heard, "Delilah, who's that?"

"Just a friend, mum," I shouted back.

"Well let them in, don't leave them standing out in the cold."

I smiled, "Would you like to come in?"

"You know what, don't mind if I do," Christopher said as he smirked.

"Mum, this is Christopher. He's a friend from school," I said.

"Well perhaps he should stay for tea," she said.

"Oh, I don't think..." I said, hesitating, as I tried to think of an answer for him not to stay.

"That would be lovely, Mrs. Bloom, thank you," said Christopher.

"Dinner will be served at 6:oo pm," my mum said.

With that, I took his hand and catapulted up the stairs to my bedroom before my parents had the chance to ask what I would consider embarrassing questions. We spent the remaining time together, lying watching TV. Soon I found myself resting my head on his shoulder, as I placed my hand firmly on his muscular chest. Twirling his fingers gently and softly as they ran through my hair as he played with it. I could feel my eyes becoming heavy, that's when I heard the fog-horn shout that dinner was ready.

"Delilah," he whispered, "I think your mum is shouting on you."

I moaned, "Do we have to move? I'm so comfy," I said, as I snuggled more into his shoulder.

"Come on," he said as he shrugged his shoulders in order to get me to move.

I lay there a bit longer.

That's when he kissed me on the forehead and said, "I don't want to be late for storytelling."

I continued to protest, trying to drag him back on the bed to lay with me.

"'If you don't move I will lift you," he said.

"You wouldn't dare!" I exclaimed.

"I believe that is a dare," he walked towards me and scooped me up.

My hands clasped at his neck. "I told you I would, now should we go downstairs," he said.

"If you put me down first," I said.

He put me down and we walked downstairs. I could tell my parents were eagerly waiting to ask the questions I was hoping most to avoid. We all sat down and from the first question I knew the 'few' questions my parents had would turn into an interrogation.

"So, Christopher, how do you and Delilah know each other?" asked my mum.

I looked at my dad as if to say come on make her stop but his body language told me I was on my own.

"Mum," I said as I spoke up, "I already told you he's a friend from school."

"Well, actually, Mrs. Bloom, Delilah and I were in a few of the same classes when we started high school," Christopher said.

I looked at Christopher confused, "Were we?"

"Yeah," he said as he laughed, "you were in my P.E, English and Science classes but as the years went on we were split. Until this year when we were put in the same classes, R.E and English."

"So, Mrs. Bloom, I have to ask, do you have any stories of Delilah when she was younger?" asked Christopher.

"Well, there was this one time..."

I quickly interrupt. "No mum, please not that story," I said as I pleaded for her not to tell it.

"Please, I would love to hear it," pleaded Christopher as he placed his hand on my thigh.

"It's either the story or the baby pictures," insisted my mum.

It was in that moment I felt as though the two of them were ganging up on me.

My mum continued to tell him the story; "There was this one time when Delilah's dad and I had taken her on a trip to this park where you can fish. Anyway, she had a net and held onto the tree. I don't know what happened but the next thing I know she was in there swimming with the fish!"

"No, that's not what happened," I said as I laughed and held Christopher's arm. "Actually, I had a net but I had one arm around the tree. There was a fish in front of me, and I reached to get it and as I did I ended up falling in with the fish. My mum, not rushing to my rescue, just stood there laughing."

"I bet you felt refreshed after that," he said as he laughed.

By the time the other stories had been told everyone had finished their dinner. That's when Christopher started to pile his plates in a neat pile.

"It's okay," I said as I placed my hand on his, "You don't need to do that."

I could see from the corner of my eye that my mum doubted Christopher's title of just friends.

"I just think it's the least I could do considering your parents cooked us this lovely meal."

"Well," my dad said, "the least you could do is wash up."

"Urgh, okay, yeah, we will," I said.

My parents left the table meanwhile I started to gather the neat pile of cluttered plates and glasses. I looked away for a moment to find the sink was overflown with bubbles.

"Have you washed dishes before?" I said as I laughed, "I think you don't have enough bubbles there."

"You're right. Here-" he said as he grabbed me from behind with one hand and used his other to dip his hand into the bubbles. I tried to fight against his strength but I couldn't, he wiped my face with them. I then grabbed some myself and tried to put some on him but he was too strong. I found myself under his chin in his lean frame.

"Do you give up yet?" he asked.

I smiled and laughed, "Okay, fine... Yes, I give up."

He let go of my hands, my hands still full of bubbles I grabbed his face and pulled him close to me to kiss, leaving the taste of my gloss to linger on his lips.

After our fight with the bubbles, it was time for Christopher to go home.

He held out his hand, "Thank you, Mr. and Mrs. Bloom for the dinner, it was a pleasure."

"You should come by again, Christopher," said my mum.

"Okay, mum, I think Christopher has to get home," I said as I practically shoved him out.

Standing on the doorstep I said in a joking manner, "So did you enjoy tonight then?"

"I look forward to it again as a matter of fact," he said as he smirked.

He then came in close, gave me a hug and kissed me on the cheek, "Goodnight Delilah." He proceeded to walk away into the distance.

· · ·

It had been a few hours now and I still hadn't heard from him. No phone call or text, I would refresh my Facebook every few minutes to see if he had messaged me, but nothing. He was even online a few times but he just ignored my messages. I didn't understand what was happening. I thought everything was okay between us. Maybe I'm naive. Maybe I'm the problem.

It was just another day at school, and I could see him amongst the crowd at his locker. I was walking down the corridor and there he was at his locker. I decided to get some answers. Fighting my way towards him against the stampede.

"Hey, Christopher!" I shouted amongst the crowd.

He glanced in my direction. He picked up his bag as he slammed his locker door closed and proceeded to walk away.

"Hey, Christopher," I said as I smiled.

He was silent and reserved.

"Have I done something wrong?" I asked.

He paused for a brief second. "I just... I just think we should be friends," he said.

I promised myself I wouldn't let my emotions get the best of me, but I could feel a lump in my throat, "What? Why?" I asked, as my voice broke with devastation.

He sighed and clenched his jaw, "I just think we shouldn't be together. Yesterday was a mistake," he said.

I felt my heart fall to my feet; it was a tragic mess, broken into pieces. Meanwhile, he couldn't even look at me in the face. That told me all I needed to know.

"I don't understand... yesterday everything was fine. What happened to liking me for three years?" I asked.

"I did. But then when we got together the spark vanished. I'm sorry but I think it's best this way, not just for me but for both of us. We got in too deep too quick," he said.

I tried to grab onto his arm. "I don't believe that's the real reason. Tell me what I've done wrong," I cried.

He pulled his arm away and sighed, "You want the truth? It just wasn't working out. I find myself better without you."

I slid down the lockers and fell to the corridor floor hall as he walked away.

And in that last moment, I felt a wave of emotion surged through me. They crashed upon the shore, showering me with cold, frozen water as a fresh river of tears misted my eyes and tickled at my waterline. I was left with my tortured mind questioning everything I ever said and done, thinking it was my fault. Could I fix things? Perhaps; I could make things right if I just apologise. Maybe we could be together again. As the week went on the days just became 'just another one' that I blended into the background. As I leaned against my locker I could see him, my eyes lusted for him as my thirst craved for his attention. That's when I saw another girl walk up to him and kiss him on the cheek. I guessed he moved on quick, that 'we' and 'I' didn't mean anything to him.

My heart ticked away like a bomb, surrounded by silence, it fell like a feather. Only I could hear the shattered pieces of my broken heartbreak. I saw him walk hand and hand with that other girl, that wasn't me. My mind tortured me as questions spun around in my mind. What did she have that I didn't? Why wasn't I enough? Why was I so easy to forget? Did I mean anything? But then when I saw her everything made sense, she was good for his reputation. She was someone and I was a no–one.

I knew it wouldn't have lasted but in some way, I just wished he hadn't led me on. Maybe then I wouldn't be as hurt as I am. I can't help but feel that there's just an emptiness; a hole where my heart used to be. That's when I could feel an icy grip clenched tightly around my heart. It felt as though only for a moment it had turned transparent. That when people looked at me they could see through the hole in my chest where my heart used to beat, for only him.

I guess that's the problem for a hopeless romantic wearing your heart on your sleeve. My stomach dropped as my world was demolished; everything I had come to know in my world had now collapsed. Leaving only myself standing alone as not a moment elapsed. It was as if every time I closed my eyes the memories played on a movie screen like a broken record.

I missed the little things, seeing his name light up on my phone because that's how it all started. I miss the endless conversations we would have late into the night. I miss the smile that he gave me. I miss that weird feeling I used to get whenever I would hear his voice or see him, my stomach swarming with butterflies. That rush of excitement just thinking about him. I miss us.

I deleted all the pictures. I even deleted him from my Facebook but I couldn't bring myself to delete his number or the texts. It had only been a few months since we had gone our separate ways. I was just beginning to forget about him. That was until his name popped up on my phone. I wasn't so sure I could answer it, never mind try to force myself through a conversation with him. But I couldn't help it... I gave into the pressure of weakness and I answered it.

"Hey, how have you been?" he asked.

I couldn't help but feel compelled to lie, "Yeah... I've been good, thanks. What about yourself?"

"Delilah, I know when you're lying, what's up?" asked Christopher.

I hesitated to give him an answer, "I'm fine, and there's nothing wrong with me." I protested.

"Okay, in that case, would you like to hang out for a bit with me? I mean you don't have to if it's too awkward, I respect that," said Christopher.

I couldn't help but think I may get the opportunity for him to explain. Maybe even clear things up and stop the torturing madness he left me with. And I know I probably shouldn't have agreed but I just needed that one more draw to withstand this withdrawal.

Without thinking, I said, "It would be good to catch up. Would you like to come to my house?"

"Sure, I'll be up soon."

The goofy smile he brings out on me appeared again. Then I realised how much of a hobo I looked like. I rushed about the house trying to get ready, making sure I looked decent for him coming. The problem was I didn't know what to wear from the piles and piles of clothes I had hidden away in storage. I didn't know what to wear. I didn't know how to wear my hair. What perfume I should have on? Should be natural or cheat a little? I don't have that long to get ready! I scrambled about in my wardrobe, digging for something to wear. I finally found something! Everything was going great until... my hair decided to have a bad day. No matter what I would do it wouldn't go the way I wanted it to go. Ding-dong, went the doorbell. I quickly peeked my head around the banister to see who it was at the door. Thank god, it wasn't him. With a couple of minutes to spare I spent whatever time I had left trying to get ready.

Now ready all I had to do was wait on his arrival. A few minutes go by and there was still no sign of him. The minutes soon changed to hours. Checking my phone every two minutes just in case he tried to phone me or send a text, other than just checking the time every now and again. An hour turned into two hours, which eventually turned into several passed hours. I left him a few texts but I didn't get any reply. I checked my call log but there was nothing; there was still no sign of him as the time passed by. All dressed up, I sat waiting and waiting. Why did I think this time would have been any different?

That day I eventually came to the conclusion he wasn't showing up, he had just forgotten about our plans or didn't care enough to show up. I feel as if whatever we have it's as if sometimes we're friends, sometimes we're more than friends and other times we're strangers to each other. What happened to us? I hide the fact that I still care for him. Heck, I love him. I always will and have. No words will or can describe what he means to me.

A few weeks pass by after that 'great expectation.' I was hurting so much yet I still adored him, still cared for him. One look from him across the hall and my world stopped. And seeing him with her wasn't fair. Why isn't that me? The bell went and it was just the two of us left in the hallway. The questions of why he never showed up were itching away at me. Hesitant I walked over...

"Hey, Christopher..." I hesitantly said.

"What do you want?" he snapped.

"I just wanted to know why you didn't show up when you said you would," I said.

He closed his locker door and leaned against it. "Something came up," he said as he shrugged his shoulders.

"It's just I waited around all day, and I didn't hear anything from you. It was later on when I realised you weren't coming. I just want to know why," I said.

He sighed out of frustration, "Urgh, I... just..."

"Hey, you two!" We suddenly heard from a distance.

We looked at each other. Christopher grabbed my hand and we started to run through the hall.

"You're getting pretty good at this, skipping school," he said laughing.

"Shut up," I said smiling, "This isn't supposed to be made a habit," I said as I freaked out.

· · ·

We ended up back at my house.

"So I was thinking..." I said as I unlocked the door. "We could talk about something?"

We walked up the stairs to my bedroom.

"We could watch a movie," I said as I went to sit on my bed.

"Sure, but are your parents home?" he asked.

"No, we're all alone," I said.

"Well in that case I have an idea for something we could do to pass the time if you like," he said as he winked at me.

He wandered over to my door looking at the medals, "You won these?"

I walked over, "Yeah..." I started to point out the different medals for the things I had done.

As I talked I noticed he was glancing at me and smiling.

"What is it?" I asked curiously, thinking I had something on myself.

"Nothing," he said, smirking. "I just had an idea of what we can do."

He takes a step towards me, placing his hands on my hips. Suddenly my back is against the door. I pulled my hair bobble out, letting my hair fall gracefully. He takes my hands, holding them above my head up against the door. He then lets them go only for them to fall around his neck. In one swift movement he lifted me up, my legs wrapped around his waist, adrenaline rushed through my veins. The tension you could cut with a knife. Now all I wanted was for him to push his lips against mine. Maybe even rip off my top, as we get lost in a moment of passion, heat and sweat. He throws me on the bed. He takes his top off. I became utterly perplexed, for the first time I noticed he had that type of beauty that you only see once; maybe twice in a lifetime. The kind that really knocks you off your feet. And forces you to pinch yourself to check that you're not dreaming. The kind that you begin to fall in love with as soon as you see it. His cheeks were chiseled like a finely carved Michelangelo statue. His nose was perfectly symmetrical. His lips were slightly full: the kind that end in a cute little smirk at the corners. The rays of sun highlighted the dimples in his cheeks and chin. His lips were like sweet berries, his cologne had this strong smell that made me even more drawn to him. His eyes were big, green and dangerously daring. His frame was so firm and perfectly fit as spectacles of sweat ran down the cuts of his abs. His hair was like deep waves that I wouldn't mind entwining my hands through.

What more could a girl want? My heart beating rapidly as we passionately kissed, I found myself hanging onto every second not wanting for him to stop. I started craving more. His touch was soft and gentle, but yet strong and seductive. His breath was like steaming hot bath water as it brushed on my top lip. That's when I felt his lips tracing from my ear to my collarbone. As we fooled around more I found my top comfortably lying next to his on the floor, as we thrived with each other's company, my hair was a mess - but I didn't care. And just as things were getting good my phone started to go off.

"Don't answer it, just ignore it," he begs.

"I have to," I said, pushing my hair out of my face, "It could be an emergency."

"The only emergency you have to attend to is me," he said as rolled me on my back.

The phone continued to ring.

"As much as I'm enjoying this I need to answer my phone," I said as I kissed him.

I rolled towards my phone and quickly answered it, "Hello?" I said.

"Hi darling, are you home from school yet?" asked my mum.

"Yeah, I'm just in and doing my homework," I said.

"Okay well, your dad and I were thinking of doing pizza for dinner tonight," she said.

"Yeah, that sounds great mum. Listen, I need to concentrate on my homework. I'll see you when you come in. Bye," I said, trying to end the conversation quickly.

I got off the phone and rolled back his way. I said, "Now where were we?"

But he had already gotten up.

"I should probably go, it's getting pretty late," he said.

Putting his t-shirt back on, I walked towards him and placed my hands on his waist.

"You don't have to go," I protested.

He broke away from me and started to gather his things.

"Why are you being moody and weird with me? What just happened?"

"I'm not being moody. And I don't know, Delilah, you tell me." He sighed. "Look, it doesn't matter," he said as he tied his shoes. "It's probably just for the best if I do go," he said as he put his phone in his pocket.

He then got up and left as I was left alone to wonder what just happened. Had I done something wrong? Was it my fault? Maybe it's nothing, maybe I'm overthinking things.

My feet were exhausted from running through my mind trying to make sense of things. What did I do wrong for him to stop looking at me in that way? Now when he looks at me his eyes are filled with emptiness. Yet there are so many feelings and emotions behind the looks we used to exchange between one another. I still believe in love. I just have a hard time believing in people and their intentions for me.

I remember how he would hold his arms out to lean into me as I leaned into him. How he would pull me closer to him; as he held me tighter just as I was about to break away. I never wanted the moment to end. I felt safe in his strong arms and when he let go, I knew that the only place I wanted to be was with him.

My phone buzzes, I force myself to hold my head up. It was Christopher.

It's hard to forget about him, all the things we did and the way we touched. I gave everything. I even gave the best of myself but he didn't care to notice. No matter what we decided to do, in the end, I'm always the one who gets hurt. I get mixed signals. One minute he's flirting and the next he acts arrogant and becomes distant. Why is it him my heart so belongs to?

That night I was left defenseless against my own enemy - my mind. I kept thinking maybe, it could work. Maybe being friends with benefits with Christopher could make him fall for me or would I be setting myself up for false hope? I already knew the answer but I didn't want to admit it. I just wanted one moment where I felt we connected. Am I shallow to stoop to that level? To just know what it's like to feel his love towards me, agree to be his muse?

The next day comes and goes as I become on autopilot. I flopped on my bed as I let out a big sigh. Just as I was gathering myself together Christopher texted me.

"So have you thought about the offer?" Christopher curiously asked.

"Yeah, why not. Like you said it will be fun," I said without giving a second thought.

"Great, I'll see you tomorrow at seven o'clock."

I was nervous, my heart racing. I still made my way to his house. There he was, he opened the door. He took my hand in his and led me to his room, closing the door behind him. He took me in his arms, my back against the door. I smiled when he gently kissed me. Passionately we kissed. I ripped off his top in one swift movement. Slowly I began to feel his body. His lips moving from mine, he began tracing the lines of my ear to then my collarbone. I was in a total daze and all I cared about was how good it felt. But that did it for me; I took off my t-shirt and pressed my chest against Christopher's. He touched my body, so gently and passionately. He picked me up and threw me on the bed, climbing on top of me.

Am I going about this the right way? Something about this just doesn't feel right. Maybe this is a mistake. But I don't want to leave. I love being in his presence. I've dreamed about having a connection such as this for so long. Am I really going to throw all that away for 'the right thing to do?' Maybe I should just call it off. Am I only hurting myself? Letting him lead me on.

"Wait, Christopher..." I said, pushing myself away from him.

"What is it?" He asked as he moved to the other side of me.

"I'm sorry but I just can't... I can't go through with this. I thought I could but I can't. This was a mistake. I'm sorry. All I'm going to do is let you lead me for me to fall so deeply for you. I will only hurt myself. Our relationship, I can't even tell you what it is, it's so complicated. I don't want to be with someone this way. It isn't right."

I gathered my stuff and headed home. As soon as I got home I buried my head within my pillows to muffle the sound of my heartache.

As I fell in love with him there was some part of me telling me not to. My intuition was screaming from the inside, but I chose to ignore it. I chose to listen to my heart. I thought my heart could never be wrong. Only this time, my heart had been deceived. He was so infatuating and I couldn't help myself. But I knew I couldn't stay. I had to leave because "I love him" wasn't enough. I cared about him so much and that's what crushed me.

I have always dealt with the reality of people leaving. They will come and go like the wind. So it never surprises me when people leave me. I have never been afraid of starting over. However, it's different this time because I'm the one leaving. I respect myself too much. I make the hard decision to leave because we both deserve to be happy, even if that means I can't be with him. I probably hurt him by leaving but if it's any consolation, I hurt myself too in the process.

The truth is I left because I wasn't enough for him and that made me feel insecure. No matter what I did I was never enough. And that was the problem. I needed to know I was enough, I needed the approval. So I knew I wasn't imagining that there wasn't this 'great love' between us. Just so I could have confirmation that something was real and did exist, that it wasn't all in my head. Or perhaps, I just really wanted to know once and for all that he did want to be with me. That I wasn't right in thinking he was playing mind games and calling me whenever I seemed convenient. The hardest part about it all is somewhere deep inside of my mind, I knew what was going on. But I was in denial. Why you ask? I didn't want to accept it. I didn't want to admit he wasn't the guy who I fell in love with. So I continuously fought against the voice in my head, refusing to face the brokenness and shambles that was our 'relationship'. I gave him numerous attempts to prove me wrong when I hoped he would change... but he never did. I was hoping he wasn't just seizing the countless chances I gave him just to take advantage of my naivety. And that he did in fact love me. Was it wishful thinking when I would hope for him to wake up, to see what he was losing and someone else would gain someday.

He drained me until I had nothing left. It was exhausting. His emptiness consumed me. I was left with nothing but a shell of what was once a fun-loving girl. The emptiness started whenever he would blame me. He never wanted to admit to his actions because he never cared. I wonder if he ever felt remorse, would he ever regret the way he made me feel.

I should hate him for everything he had put me through. But I can't. So no matter what he has done, how he has made me feel, I know deep down he wasn't worthy of my love, and for that, I will never be able to hate him. All I ever needed was one thing from him. I needed him to need me; the way I thought I needed him. I wanted him to fight for me because I refused to give up on us without a fight.

I hoped 'our relationship' was at least worth fighting for, hoped he would have considered we were something valuable.

Whatever happened to the simplicity in the deeply provoking thinking we had together about everything or the exchanging intense looks. And somewhere in the midst of it, all my walls came crumbling down with just his touch. But I guess I was naive to think his had come down too. There were chambers he wasn't letting me through. I never expected him to be extraordinary, I never expected him to become something he wasn't. I accepted him just as he was. I may have been blind, but I was perfectly aware of his flaws and valued them as his strengths. His imperfections perfectly complimented my own. Even the things that drove me crazy about him, I loved.

Maybe I fell too fast. Maybe I fell too hard. But he was right there with me. He led me to believe that this was something. I believed every word because they weren't just words but actions that followed. Somewhere between clothes on the floor and his fingers running through my hair, I thought this was different. It wasn't just a physical thing, but there were emotions neither of us could deny were present. It felt different. He was different. We were different. And we would get lost in a world we made of our own, and we didn't even know how much time passed. But somewhere along the way, something had changed him.

Eyes that once adored me turned dark as they looked away. And all I wanted to do was fix it. He made me feel like an idiot because I was willing to give him a million chances. Everyone kept asking why but I saw something in him. I thought there was something there. In fact, I know there still is. Maybe all of it scared him as much as it did me. But I've believed the best things in life are the things that scare you, and those are the things you have to run towards, not run away from. With every simple touch, I could feel it from my head to my toes. From every kiss, he left me wanting more. So whenever the day comes when he is ready to fight for me, I'll be here. Because even with a broken heart, I still believe in him. I still believe that we can make it. I still want him. Unfortunately, that makes me hate him at the moment. I've never been one to wait around but I do think there are people worth waiting for.

I just wish when I was falling in love with him there were traffic lights, so I would know if I should have gone for it, slowed down, or just stopped. Because knowing I would see his face, feel his touch and hear his voice was the last time... it didn't seem fair that's how things would end. Knowing the next time I saw him would be in different circumstances.

STRANGERS ON A WINTER NIGHT

ARIK MITRA

Behind a glass window, high up on some floor of a skyscraper near Golpark, the wall-clock had ceased to tick. The minute and the hour hands had stopped close and yet short of each other; they had fallen squarely upon an hour before midnight. The city had gone under a blanket of mist, with the intention of slowly sinking deeper, below the depths of silent sleep. It was perhaps this silence that had drawn her out, aimless, and without the sanguinity of one who leaves never to return again. Winter months, a short-staying luxury, a time to be savored, had come upon the city, and the nights....the nights always trundled with a silence; a silence only the reduced visibility an obscuring December lightlessness might beget.

Quietly drowsed this giant, this urban ghost, that never quite let go of what it used to be; this myriad of condiments, that nostalgic reflection often kept bringing back without a name...but which home-coming wanderers knew in their hearts as Kolkata.

And so it happened on a night in the midst of December, that Kolkata was rhythmically rocking like an old man nodding in sleep; and the street lamps had taken their guard-post till dawn's first inklings of light, and Pritha heard nothing but the distant din of the ever sleepless urban traffic.

She could not even hear her footsteps (having worn sneakers), as she crossed the road to take the pavement opposite to Rabindra Sarovar Metro Station. The evening had gone by, missed by the restless yet exhausted submissiveness, rooted in the uncertainty as to whether or not she should take a metro to wherever some friend had an apartment, where she could stay the night, deciding upon the next course of action. But in the end, she had decided against it. By the time the first morning light crept up to the steps flanking the closed shutters of shops, her family would already have scoured half of the city in her search. If she had to go, it had to be somewhere outside the city. Somewhere she would get enough time to think her next steps thoroughly through. Hence the airport. Whatever flight to whatever city. She had friends here and there. Some colleagues too. It would buy her sufficient time.

Some guys on motorbikes near the gate of the metro station were looking at Pritha as she crossed the road, whispering between themselves. They wore covid masks, their hidden faces looking all the more menacing, effusing some unseemly intention. She could still feel their eyes on her, as she made her way on the opposite pavement, towards a side street she meant to take. Pritha suddenly felt colder. She took off her mask and tried to wrap her jacket even tighter, her fast-paced breath condensing into vapor as soon as exhaled. The streets were becoming quieter and quieter. A dog howled from afar. Pritha walked aimlessly. Cold sweeps of wind hit her face. She hadn't cried all this time out of a heaviness in her heart. But the wind brought her to tears quite easily. She had left home that evening. Left never to return again. It had not been a very planned action; she was having one of her bouts of severe depression and had originally left to go somewhere to get fresh air. Maybe somewhere out of Kolkata for a few days to get out of the city life. But as evening gave way to night, she felt more and more ill at ease.

The streetlamps stared hard, lapping up her entire silhouette with their dim unearthly eyes. She felt exposed; picked up her pace. It is when turning to an even quieter and mist-cloaked side street, that her field of vision picked up a moving shadow from the corner of her left eye. She didn't stop. She didn't increase her pace. Instead, she entered the side street she had intended to take and walked further for a few more meters. Then, without notice, suddenly jolted around as soon as she could make out faint footsteps turning at the corner. A tall coated silhouette could be seen vaguely in the smoky mist. Pritha felt a surge of irritation foaming out from inside her. "Why the hell are you following me sala?!", she shouted out, her voice bouncing off the concrete of the sleeping streets. The tall fellow wasn't expecting such a sudden retort. He stood dead still for a moment. Then Pritha heard a muffled laugh, one of childlike notoriety. The tall figure amusedly said, "You have dropped your metro card. I had even called out to you once. But you seemed so absentminded, you didn't notice and that got me intrigued" He continued to speak as he got closer, "What's the case? Run away from home?"

No response came immediately to Pritha's mind. She felt a pang of caution hit her beneath the ribs. But the fellow's words had something in them. He did not feel like someone very dangerous. Even if he was, there was little Pritha could do under the circumstances. She decided to go ahead and answer. She had been taking chances all evening anyway, ever since stepping out of her house. "Yes, so what's it to your father?!", she hissed at him. The fellow did not seem offended by the answer. He slowly walked closer to Pritha, in an energetic gait. As he came into view, Pritha could see a sly smile on his face, peeking for moments from inside his high collared coat. He calmly answered in a matter-of-fact manner, "Oh nothing! Absolutely nothing! My father has gone over the fence a long time ago", chuckling as he finished. "So, why'd you run away?" he added.

Pritha was looking at him, thinking if she should deny it. The fellow had a subtle smile still stuck to his face. Suddenly he said, "Thinking about denying it?" Pritha was taken aback. Who was this man? How could he know what she was thinking? She thought for a moment, frowned, and then let out a sigh. What was the point anyway? She answered in a hopeless tone,

"Yes. I ran away." The man's smile slowly subsided and now showed unexpected hints of annoyance.

"And?"

Pritha stared stupidly, not able to catch his meaning.

"And what?"

"What are you going to do now? What's the plan?"

Pritha felt puzzled. Going to the airport and catching a plane was her initial idea. As to where she would go, she would decide on her way to the airport. Things had appeared rather lucid once the idea of going to the airport had come to her. Now, she was not so sure. The man looked at her with steady eyes, waiting for her answer. That she was now befuddled, annoyed Pritha. Her anger went towards the man for bringing it up. She fumed at him,

"What's it to you!".

The man didn't wait. Neither did he respond. He simply took Pritha's right arm and thrust the metro card onto her palm. His grip was strong as steel and warm. After handing over the card, he simply took off from whence he came, in the opposite direction. As she watched him go, Pritha felt ill at ease. She waited a few more moments, but he did not turn back; nor did he lower his pace. In a flash of utter helplessness, she called out to him.

"Please wait! Don't go off! Wait!"

The man seemed to slow down a bit. Pritha almost ran up to take his side. The night grew dense and fell like black viscous liquid upon their sleeves and down their half-covered faces. Pritha now walked in a steady gait. It was hard to keep up with the man, his tall legs taking immense strides across the dewy footpath.

"So what are you doing, walking about the streets at night, dressed like some villain out of a crime thriller?" She asked.

The man did not hesitate the least bit in his reply, "I had just finished up business and was going to get something to eat..." He did not finish his sentence, his mind wandering off to some unknown alley, far beyond what Pritha deemed fathomable .

Then he suddenly asked her, "Have you eaten anything?"

"No."

"Very good. Let's go eat", and he started walking again. His long legs seemingly traversed a meter in one go. Once again Pritha found it difficult to keep up with him. Coming to his side, she asked again,

"You didn't answer my question. What are you doing this time of night dressed like this?"

"But I did. I said I had just finished up work and was going to get something to eat"

"What kind of work requires dressing up like this? That is what I'd like to know."

"Oh! I madam, am an artist. One from an almost dying art. Dying upon the breast of Kolkata."

"What is that? Sculpture?"

"Arey no no. Absolutely not! My art has nothing to do with standing figures, but with living, moving figures!"

"And what is that?"

"I, am a pickpocket"

"Bah bah, beautiful! And you're saying that with such confidence!"

"Why not!"

Pritha found herself wanting to laugh, in spite of it all. But instead, she now thought it would really be great if she could get something to eat. She hadn't eaten anything since morning and now, at almost midnight, was the first time that she felt genuine hunger. And she felt a sudden lightness. Though she actually hadn't laughed, she had felt, even if momentarily, her heaviness go away. And it hadn't come back.

"O, Madam!"

Pritha came back to her senses. She stared blankly at the man walking next to her. He was saying something. He was saying, "You look rich. Dinner won't be anything special. Will be lucky if Pocha Da manages anything at all."

Pritha felt intrigued. This was all very new to her. "Pocha Da? Is that a name?" she asked.

The man was surprised. "What do you mean?", he stared dumb-founded at her. Then suddenly a smile came upon his lips. "Seems like you're way too rich. Maybe I should have just nipped you instead."

Pritha gave him a dissolving stare. He laughed, "No no. I'm just joking!". Then he laughed again, this time a little cautious, at which Pritha burst out freely... her first free laughter in what appeared to be weeks.

And the night quietly crept down the tree-trunks; from dark gatherings between the leaves; from beneath the hazy light of streetlamps and walked quietly beside them; and the silence eloquently spoke through the gap between them, as the two souls walked in search of nourishment, denied by the chilling dew. But what were they indeed searching? What were they indeed walking toward? What except their own little worlds waiting to burst forth, one upon the other. And so silence spoke in their ears and set forth just the right moment amongst the innumerable of time and space that would allow them to pour out those frothing tales inside their hearts.

"So what's the case?" he spoke first.

Pritha found the question rather puzzling, now that she tried to actually form an explicable answer inside her head. Why had she run away from home? Did she want freedom? Freedom from what? Monotony?

Pritha quickly realised that the answers were beyond her reach. She said, "I don't really know. I was having a bout of severe depression and just felt like running away from it all."

"Hmm. Won't your parents be looking for you?"

"They probably already are, with all their big shot contacts."

"Then we better be careful. Come with me", the man entered a blind alley near Esplanade. Pritha recognized the place to be Esplanade because she could spot the Grand Hotel on Chowringhee, far away from them though it was. Walking for some more time, a vague light could be seen in the distance. The overcoat spoke again,

"See there, that is Pocha Da's stall".

The stall was closed. There was a heap in an old worn-out blanket lying flat on the table of the stall. The light that could be seen in the distance was a dim bulb hanging from a wooden beam above the heap. The overcoat went straight and knocked on the blanket heap like it some door.

"Pocha Da! Pocha Da! Get up!" There was some moaning from under the blanket. A rusty voice grumbled,

"Which scoundrel is it now? In the damn middle of the night!"

Pritha saw it again. That smile. That spark of childlike notoriety. He grinned and said,

"Arey, your saviour my dear Pocha Da. Now get up"

The blanket stirred and a figure came out of it. The man was quite tall. And old. He had been lying with his arms and legs folded and hence had fit the small table. "Arey, it's you. Have a seat. Have a seat." Pocha Da brought out some newspapers. The two of them sat on them. It was very chilly. Pritha drew closer. He was emanating a sort of comfortable warmth. Out of the overcoat, came a bottle of neat whiskey. Pocha Da's eyes glinted. Enthusiastically he asked,

"Is it foreign or Indian?"

"Foreign. Foreign. Even your father never had stuff like this before. Now, what's for dinner?"

"What else at this time of night? Some maggi with onions and green chili."

"First class. Get to it. Give me three glasses in the meantime."

Pritha watched them go at amazing speed. Within ten minutes the elderly man had cooked maggi for three of them, serving it piping hot on edge-broken plates. The whiskey seemed to be gleaned from the night itself, the mist laden yellow having gathered like droplets dripping from the orange streetlight at the mouth of the lane. Pritha hesitated. At one point she said,

"I've never had alcohol like this before. It was always in 5-stars before this."

To this, the man simply said, "Well, you've never run away from home before either," and took a draught from his glass. Old Pocha Da was really enjoying his drink. He ate and drank very slowly; sitting a little further away from the two of them; savoring each drop. He already seemed drunk. Pritha felt sightly dizzy herself after having finished the first glass. She felt warm inside. The alcohol gave her courage and helped her relax. She now asked the man sitting beside her something she had been wanting to all night.

"You said you're a pickpocket. Don't you get frustrated with this kind of life? Not feel bad about all the things you could have been? Could have done? Rich perhaps....." her voice trailed off as she drowned in a warm sleepiness from her second glass of whiskey. The answer she received brought her out of trance.

"No, not really. Pickpocket I did not want to be, yes. But then who can ever know what he or she becomes. I did what I had to survive. What I could have been doesn't bother me at all. Things are going well now. South Kolkata is full of rich people. Heh heh."

"Aren't you afraid of getting caught?", Pritha asked.

"Of course! But that's the fun of it," the man finished his drink. Pritha fell silent. However meager, however strange, these people seemed to have something even the very rich like her didn't. This was the first time she didn't feel cuddled in the arms of comfort. The first time she felt life was staring at her hard in the face. She felt alive. Yes..that was the word...Alive. They were already on their feet and making way towards the main road. Then she heard his voice from the overcoat say,

"Well, the night will somehow pass. But the morning? Where will you go?"

Pritha did feel like thinking about these things right now. She lazily waved him off saying,

"Oh, just drop me somewhere near the airport. Don't talk about that now!"

"And where will you go?", he added.

"Oh somewhere. We'll decide that later. Shut up now. Let's go somewhere", Pritha returned.

But they could not keep talking. Just as they came upon the main road, a speeding car came at furious throttle from the direction of Park Street. It skidded for some distance, barely missed hitting them and went off like a misfired rocket towards Bentinck Street. Pritha had momentarily froze and held him tight, closing her eyes. The awkward silence between them after that was short-lived. They heard a muffled scream come from the direction of Bentinck Street. Pritha frightened, asked,

"What was that?"

"I think someone's been run over. Let's go and see"

"No no. I can't see that. You go and see. I'll wait."

"It will be fine. Come with me," He took Pritha by the arm and ran....

A man lay bloodied just off the corner where Bentinck Street led to China Bazaar. One of his feet had broken. Evidently, a car tire had gone over it. He had been sleeping on the pavement.

Pritha felt a shivering cold run through her. She was paralysed. A surge came upon her. A surge of profound grief. She was sinking...sinking further....when suddenly a jolt! Her head to toe felt shaken. He was shaking her,

"Madam! O, Madam! You alright? Snap out of it!"

Pritha felt herself gradually coming to. Words came unsteady out of her mouth,

"I was...having...another episode"

"Don't worry. Everything's fine. I'm here." and so it was. Pritha looked wide-eyed.

"Now let's get this man to the hospital. There's one close by."

He lifted the man on his shoulder and went off. Pritha followed him in silence. She did not feel as scared anymore. The alcohol had worn off due to the episode, but she now felt calm.

It was Pritha who got the injured fellow admitted to the hospital. She even paid for his stitches. He would be released the day after. Overcoat was out of sight. Naturally, since police could often be seen around hospitals at this hour.

As she came out of the hospital, Pritha saw the world in a new light. It was the first time in her life that she had done something for anyone, without any expectations. It felt so liberating, that she couldn't help but smile to herself. She could see him standing at a distance on the opposite pavement. As she reached him, he suddenly said

"How about we go to the Ganges!"

"Eh! Ganges at this time in winter?!"

He thought for a second or two. Then with childlike excitement looked at Pritha with big eyes and added,

"Why not. Let's go!" Pritha gave in.

"How long a way is it from where?"

"Oh, it's long. But let's go anyway. I'll manage something"

And so he did; miraculously opening a lock on a bicycle and stealing it from in front of a random house in a lane near Lalbazar crossing.

And off they went. Two shadows into the blind hours of night. Both in search of something. And yet just as pleased at not finding it. Both going somewhere. But just as happy for not having reached there...

A veil of mist wrapped around them like a shawl on the Ganges bank; obscuring them from their conscious selves of material existence. They were like phantasms, closely gathered mounds of mist, drawn to each other like distant lamps on a foggy night, like a lost ship at sea to the warm rays of a lighthouse; and they sat quietly breathing out vaporous breath...carrying what all parts of themselves they would never know. For who in history has measured his share in the quiet exchange of hearts on the banks of a river on a moonless night? Who can know how much is given and how much is received?

And they did not know. They did not measure. They did not care. They simply sat beside each other, without a sound; watching the river slowly whirl its mist; bring the lights from buildings on the other side in view and the very next second, cover them again in overlying cloaks of cloud; it was a hide and seek of meanings, a hide and seek of emotions, of vices, of virtues, all brought forth into urban frames on the eternal canvas some long dead unknown painter.

He spoke first,

"You know. It's strange for the likes of us....who do not have a home. Even if rooted inside....we still float about."

Pritha felt a pang. A sudden warmth poured inside her heart. She simply said,

"What if you had a home?"

He looked at her. They kept looking into each other's eyes. Seconds passed. Then he laughed.

"Madam, one born without a rope cannot be tied anywhere for too long," "And besides.....," he didn't finish.

Pritha knew what he meant to say. But still, she asked, "Besides?"

He didn't answer.

Pritha found her eyes slowly coming down with heavy lids. The night had been eventful, even wonderful if one could call it that...but also exhausting for her. She leaned on his shoulder and slowly sunk into sleep. As she descended into the world of dreams, she could vaguely hear him saying something. But she couldn't stay awake long enough to listen to what it was.

Sounds of morning served to wake her in place of the alarm clock she used at home. Crows, the eddies in the water, people's voices. She found herself covered with a piece of cloth as she sat up and yawned. Looked like a torn piece of blanket. The waters of the Ganges shined in the morning sunlight. People had already come to the ghats to bathe. Bells from some distant temple could be heard. Pritha stood up when her eyes went to her finger. Her ring had been restored to its place. The ring she thought she had thrown away in despair, in Esplanade when they were having a drink. She thought no one had noticed. That damned pickpocket...... She cried. Tears came without a wind this time. She cried endlessly. And she laughed......She laughed sitting inside the taxi that was taking her home. She had only come out to get some fresh air. In its stead, she had found what she perhaps needed much more than fresh air.......she had found warmth.

THE AGELESS ART OF DATING

SHARI HELD

Nate Mason squeezed his eyes shut behind his tortoiseshell glasses and jabbed the return key. There, he'd done it. Sent his completed questionnaire. A five-hundred-word essay laying out his entire life to strangers. He'd had to stretch his bona fides to come up with that much.

Maybe he shouldn't have included skydiving. He'd only done it once, and that was by mistake. His cousin, the intended skydiver, asked Nate to go along for the ride, then conveniently chickened out and volunteered Nate to take his place. If Nate hadn't read the instruction booklet to coach his cousin, they'd still be picking pieces of him off the landscape.

But it was part of his dating essay now. And it did give it some pizazz. He wasn't kittenfishing, after all. He'd skydived once. No need to mention he'd rather paint a red clown smile on his face in permanent marker than do a repeat.

A young hotshot entrepreneur with a six-digit savings account, Ferrari, and penthouse apartment overlooking Lake Michigan, Nate was not. He'd consider himself lucky to find a date with a jones for an average-looking twenty-five-year-old retail manager who drove a

2010 Dodge Neon and lived in a respectable neighborhood in the Windy City.

And how many babes would put that in their dream date description?

His best bud Kip had goaded Nate into applying to a dating service. Finally, he'd caved, although he'd opted for the cheapest one – Dream Dates R Us. The setup struck Nate as odd. Only females and people identifying as female could see the photos and read the bios of prospective dates. For males, it was a leap of faith into the abyss of blind dating. At any rate, his profile officially resided in their database populated with – if you could believe their hype – info on hundreds of other millennial hopefuls. He'd probably have better results if he hired one of those matronly matchmakers.

Nate figured his odds at success were as slim as his savings account. But, maybe, just maybe, he'd find someone nice. Ah, who was he kidding? He was as interesting as the three soggy, Splenda packets on a nearby table.

Kip burst through Starbucks' door, a grin on his face as wide as a crescent moon. It was unusual for Kip to rise before eleven on Saturdays. Something must be up.

"Hey, you go through with it?"

"Yep. They promise three meet-and-greets within the first week." That's three more than he'd landed in the last three months, but Nate wasn't going to share this sad statistic with Kip.

Kip slapped him on his back. "Way to go! You'll be knee-deep in chicks before you know it. Hey, you should bring one of them to our football party next Sunday."

Nate checked his watch, then stood and grabbed his computer. "We'll see. Look, I gotta run. I volunteered to work at the animal shelter today. Wanna come with me?"

"Nah, I'd rather check out the cute barista, not Lassie. Catch you later."

———

The next day Nate was brushing his teeth when he received a text notification. It was Dream Dates R Us announcing he'd been selected by one Rachel Davis who wanted to meet him at Barney's Bar at six o'clock Monday night.

Hmm. That was fast. Maybe that service is legit after all, despite its bargain price.

The location was a surprise. Barney's was old-school. Not trendy. Maybe Rachel didn't want to be seen with him in the place she usually hung out until she'd vetted him. Made sense. He accepted, then sorted through the shirts strewn around his bedroom floor, smelling the armpits until he found something acceptable. He hung it on a hanger and spritzed it with Downy Wrinkle Releaser, one of the best inventions ever. That done, there wasn't much else left to do. It's not like he could bone up on Rachel's bio and mention things they had in common. He'd have to wing it.

I hope she's not into skydiving!

By the end of the Sunday night football game, Nate received two more notifications. He was pumped. Three meet-and-greets already. He strutted around his living room in his BVDs and mimicked the Tom Cruise move from *Risky Business*. He had it! Yup! He was hot stuff!

Maybe he'd take up spelunking next. Illinois had some famous caves. The closest he'd been to one was a *AAA Traveler Magazine* he'd read in his doctor's office. But he just might give it a shot. Right now, he felt as if anything was possible.

———

Ten minutes to six on Monday night. Barney's neon sign flickered, and occasionally the "e" and "y" blacked out altogether. The heavy wood door had more gashes and dings than a crash test dummy. Inside, the light was dim. And despite Illinois' smoke-free policy, Nate could swear he detected a faint smokey haze and an occasional waft of pipe tobacco.

"Yoo-hoo," said a plump, gray-haired lady in rhinestone-trimmed cat eyeglasses, as she motioned for Nate to come to her corner of the bar.

Hmm. *My date must be in the ladies' room and asked this woman to watch out for me. That was thoughtful of her.* Nate was feeling better about this meet-and-greet already.

The woman grasped his hand and pumped his arm up and down. "My, you are a fine-looking morsel. I could just eat you up. Maybe with some whipped cream on top." She waggled her eyebrows suggestively while her eyes traveled down to his crotch. "I'm Rachel. But you already knew that, right?"

Nate's mouth hung open. He grabbed her drink and gulped it down, then coughed so hard he feared his lunch might make an appearance.

Rachel pulled a hankie out of her bosom and proceeded to wipe his mouth. Then she snapped her fingers. "Wally, get me a glass of water over here. Pronto."

Nate drained the water glass and thanked Rachel in a squeaky voice.

My god. How did I get fixed up with this over-sexed cougar? Is this a joke? Could Kip be behind this?

"If you like, I can give you mouth-to-mouth resuscitation. By training, I'm a nurse. Been retired for almost twenty years, but I wouldn't mind practicing on you."

Nate did some quick thinking. Obviously Dream Dates R Us had screwed up. It was supposed to be a service for millennials. On the other hand, Rachel may have fudged on her age, by about a hundred years. But hey, his Grandma Mason had been a pistol, too. She'd probably have liked Rachel. Heck, she probably would have gone out trolling for men with her. But Gran would stick to men closer to her own age. At least he hoped so.

"Thanks, Rachel, but I don't think that will be necessary."

"Shucks!" Her eyes twinkled. "Can't blame a girl for trying."

Nate cleared his throat. "You know, I think there's been a mix-up at Dream Dates R Us. I'm supposed to be in a database for millennials."

Rachel drooped. "Well, I figured it was too good to be true when I ran across your profile. You'll want to be getting along now. Go to some swanky bar crammed with gorgeous young women."

"Not necessarily." Nate nodded at the backgammon board on the bar. "I play a mean game of backgammon. How about you?"

Rachel smacked the table with her palm. "You're on!"

Ten games and five potent Manhattans later, Nate stumbled home. Before he crashed, he added one item to his to-do list for Tuesday – contact Dream Dates R Us.

———

"I am so, so sorry, Mr. Mason," the chirpy voice said, not sounding in the least bit sorry. "I've checked into your complaint, and I believe I've tracked down what happened. We provide a separate dating service for seniors. The two databases are differentiated by the order of the surname and first name. Seniors are denoted by surname comma first name. Millennials by first name comma surname. Your name was listed as Mason comma Nathaniel instead of Nathaniel comma Mason. Does that make sense?"

"Sure." How else are you going to answer a question like that? If he said "no" he'd get a repeat. "When can you fix it?"

"We'll take you out of the senior database right away and cancel all your pending requests. You've only agreed to three meet-and-greets so far, and you met the first one last night, right?"

"Right."

"What do you want me to do about the other two? I can call them and cancel if you like."

"Yes" was on the tip of his tongue, but it came out of his mouth as "no." He remembered the look in Rachel's eyes when she thought he was going to dump her. Given the same situation, he wouldn't want anyone doing that to his gran.

He cleared his throat. "No. I'll honor my commitment to those two." He hoped he wouldn't run into anyone he knew while he fulfilled his last two dates. Especially not Kip. He shuddered. He'd never live down the humiliation if Kip found out he was schmoozing with seniors.

"Thank you for using Dream Dates R Us, Mr. Mason. I'm delighted we could resolve your problem. Good day."

The chirper hung up on him.

Geez. This is what I get for choosing the cheapest option.

———

"So, how'd your Dream Date go?" Kip asked while they were on the pickleball court. "More importantly, was she hot?"

"You could say that." *If you count the hot flash she'd loudly announced as she held a cup of ice to her forehead.*

"Get any action? Or at least a second date?"

Nate shook his head. "Rachel was too much into games. Nice. But not my type."

"Happens. You've still got two more shots this week. And like that Meatloaf dude my dad listens to says, "Two out of three ain't bad.""

Maybe. But considering his next two would be golden agers, Nate would end up with zip out of three. And that wasn't great no matter how you tweaked the math.

"When are you seeing Dream Date Number 2?"

"Wednesday." *Please don't ask anything else.*

"You get a photo of these chicks before you meet them, right?"

"Nope. Only the women get photos. Kind of a weird arrangement, but, hey." Nate shrugged his shoulders, then slapped a ball into Kip's court, hoping that would end the discussion.

Kip let it fly by. "Doesn't matter much, anyway. There's so much catfishing going on these days. You don't know what to believe. At least an in-person meeting gives you something concrete to work with."

Nate's eyes opened wider. "That's more reflective thinking than I've ever seen out of you. Stud that you are, it sounds like you may have used a dating service." *Now, that would be a choice.*

"No way. But I've heard stories about dates gone awry. People who don't match up to their photos. Hey, do you want me to give you an emergency call with Dream Date Number 2? Get you off the hook if the date's a dud?"

"Nah. I'll be okay. Now, cut it with the third degree and play ball."

———

The parking lot of the Ten Pins Bowling Alley was packed. Nate circled twice before he got lucky and claimed a newly vacated space, beating out three other cars. He stepped inside and faced a bevy of blue hairs. Allison Wilson would be wearing a red rose tucked behind one ear. Shouldn't be too difficult to find – if he could wade through the throng of gray-haired grannies in sync with his every movement.

"Nice butt." Nate heard one say, followed by a chorus of titters. He walked the length of the bowling alley. Not a red rose in any nook and cranny. He'd been five or ten minutes late because of the parking situation. Surely she wouldn't have left. But unless she was in the Ladies Room – and no way in Hell was he going to poke his nose in there – she'd stood him up. He'd been rejected, sight unseen! He didn't know whether to be insulted or relieved.

Finally, the "nice butt" woman came over to him. "You looking for Allison?"

He nodded his head.

"I'm Cindy. Allison can't make it. Her son, who lives in Evanston, had a hip replacement and she went to help him. Turns out the big baby needs her to stay there longer than she anticipated."

Nate figured a little white lie was in order. "I'm sorry to hear that."

"She didn't want you to be disappointed, so she asked us to keep you company."

Good grief. Now he'd be dating a bowling team of blue-haired babes. Four faces looked at him expectantly. He wasn't sure he was up to it. Bowling wasn't his thing. These ladies would probably beat his socks off. And that would leave his bare feet in those stinky rental bowling shoes. Yuck!

Nate's phone buzzed and he checked it. Kip. The emergency call he hadn't asked for. Should he, or shouldn't he? He let it go to voicemail and put his phone back in his pocket. He turned to the group. "I'm game. But I have to warn you, I'll probably bring your score down."

"And our blood pressure – and spirits – up," one granny said, followed by her companions' snickers.

Between games they downed countless plastic cups of beer and munched on a never-ending supply of popcorn. Surprisingly, they won. Even with Nate on their team. As he was walking out the door, Cindy put her arm around him and said, "You're okay, kid. Any girl would be lucky to have a nice guy like you."

Instead of his usual reply to his mother – 'Yes, but there's no demand for nice guys these days' – Nate smiled and said, "Thank you."

———

Thursday night Nate met Kip at TGI Fridays for their weekly after-work beer. Nate had been dreading it all day. He was sure Kip would ask him about yesterday's meet-and-greet. And he was right.

"So, how'd it go last night? Was this one a winner?"

"Not exactly. She got called away at the last minute. But I schmoozed with four of her friends."

"Super! Four chicks instead of one! The odds are in your favor. You can't tell me not one of them would be worth seeing again."

Nate wasn't about to divulge that "hens" would be the correct terminology. He cleared his throat. "Trust me, there wasn't a girl-friend candidate among them."

Kip cocked his head, laid a hand on Nate's shoulder, and asked, "Have you ever thought you might be too picky? It's not like you're obligated to marry her or anything. Well, you've got one more chance. They say third time's a charm." He raised his drink. "Cheers!"

Nate raised his as well. But he had nothing to cheer about. His third meet-and-greet was another granny. And, unless Dream Dates R Us had experienced another glitch, not a single millennial had asked to meet him. What was wrong with him that he couldn't attract anyone younger than fifty? He ordered another drink and watched Kip flirt with a trio of stunning women as if he'd known them since childhood. Every one of their laughs was like a knife to his heart. Why couldn't he be like Kip? He shook his head. Dating. It was an art that eluded him.

On Saturday, Kip would meet up with a sexy young looker – not a day over twenty-five – and they'd drink and dance the night away while Nate would escort someone's grandmother to a tearoom. He kicked the bar – a perfunctory kick, not hard enough to scuff his shoe – chugged the rest of his beer, and signaled Kip he was heading out. Saturday at two o'clock on the dot Nate stood in front of Henrietta Lane's cheery red door. He brushed his pants, attempting to pick off the dog hair, but finally gave up. He'd volunteered at the animal shelter earlier. He hoped Henrietta liked dogs.

A spry-looking matron in her late sixties or early seventies responded to his knock and showed him to the living room. A young woman with eyes as blue as Lake Michigan, long honey-colored hair that framed her face, and a creamy complexion sat at one end of the couch. Henrietta settled into her armchair and nodded for Nate to sit at the other end of the couch.

"Nate, this is my granddaughter, Ella. You don't mind if she tags along with us, do you? She's new to Chicago and, being from a small rural town, is somewhat intimidated."

"Mind? No, I don't mind at all." He glanced at Ella. "It can be a bit much, even if you were born here. Trust me. Best to take it slow and get some basics – the grocery store, the mall, the bookstore, bakery – down pat first."

Ella nodded at him and smiled. She spotted the big wad of white fur on his navy pants the same time he did. "Do you have a dog or cat?" Her voice sounded like a quiet chime deep within a forest.

"No, but I'm in the market for a dog. I volunteer at the animal shelter, which is where I picked this up. I see a lot of dogs come and go. As soon as the right one appears, I'll know. And I'll be ready for him or her."

"Ella loves all little animals, don't you, dear?"

Ella blushed. "Yes. I'm staying with Grandmother for now, but once I get my own place, I plan to get a cat or two to keep me company."

"Cats are great, too. If you like, when you're ready to move, I can help you look for an apartment. Sometimes it's hard to size up a neighborhood just from seeing it. You need to know the history behind it before you make the leap into signing a lease."

Ella's cheeks bloomed the color of cotton candy. "Thank you. I'd like that."

Nate sat up taller on the sofa, his voice taking on a more assertive tone. "What kinds of hobbies or activities interest you? You'll want to be near those kinds of venues."

"I like to walk – someplace quiet, contemplative, and more in tune with nature than the popular trails. And I like the theater, although I don't attend often enough that I'd necessarily need to live nearby."

Henrietta coughed. "Speaking of entertainment, we should be leaving soon if we're going to be on time for our reservation."

"Oh, yes," Ella said. "I forgot all about the time. Sorry."

"Not to worry, dear. I do believe I am developing a headache.

They can be so beastly. Migraines, you know." She paused, then turned toward Nate. "Young man, I don't think I'll be able to accompany you to the tearoom. But Ella's been looking forward to it. Why don't the two of you go? You can tell me all about it later."

A warm feeling rushed through Nate from his head to his toes. "My pleasure," he said, rising from the couch. As he did, his jacket sleeve knocked against the side table. A business card fluttered to the carpet. Nate bent over and picked it up.

It read, Henrietta Lane, Matchmaker.

THE LAST ONE
TIM O'NEAL

CORBIN

Another lonely Sunday morning. Bored with reading, I picked up my phone, checked my emails, Reddit page, and other social media sites. With no others left to open, my fingers strayed to the Splinter dating app. I heaved a sigh. Might as well put in the time playing the game to find the love of my life.

On the internet. Yee. Haw.

A stream of toxic masculinity invaded my eyes. Camo pants. Muddy combat boots. Orange hunter caps. Muscle poses. Hairy armpits. Gross and grosser.

I kept on swiping left.

Why did all these men look the same? Didn't they have anything else besides the three basic muscle poses?

A half-dozen more profiles flashed by.

I was nearing my daily allotted swipes when I stumbled on this one guy's Splinter page. His profile picture showed him in a plaid armchair and holding a leather-bound book. His name was Mohammed. He had a lovely dark skin tone and close-cropped curly hair. His face showed a genuine smile. That alone announced his difference from all the other pasty redneck wannabes.

Intrigued, I read his bio. It was long. Kinda wordy and not exactly a thrilling read, if I'm being honest. He listed all his interests—volunteering, cooking, and the inescapable love for hiking. But it *did* lack the braggadocio tone that all the other shirtless profiles peddled.

Curious, I flipped through Mohammed's photos. One showed him in a flour-stained apron, baking cookies for a charity event. Another had him in the city library reading a picture book to kids. A hot action shot revealed well-defined cords of sweat-shiny muscles rippling along his shoulders and legs as he slam-dunked a basketball. My eyes drank in that one, but I liked his last photo best—a close-up of his handsome features. A closed-lipped smile exhibited the warmth, which radiated from his brown eyes.

I swiped back to the beginning, flipping through his photos again. Not a shirtless pic in the bunch. Nor a single dead fish either.

That was OK with me. This guy had class.

Again, I stopped on that last photo. I couldn't resist grinning back at him. I could like a man who showed his vulnerable side.

I bit my lip. A fluttering warmth stirred in my chest. My index finger tapped Mohammed on his curving lips and brushed to the right. A square blue text appeared on my screen: 'LIKED!'

Yup, I sure did. And who knows, maybe he'd like me back? That's how we played this modern dating game, right? A girl could always dream.

Another message from Splinter informed me that I'd used up all my 'LIKES' for the day and would I care to pay for an upgraded subscription?

I declined. It bothered me that all these dating services reeked of capitalism, requiring users to buy coins or starfish or beans or whatever kitschy currency they used.

Besides, I didn't mind waiting to see what happened next with that last one...

MOHAMMED

My phone pinged as I sat reading *Pride and Prejudice*. That classic novel, with its incredibly depicted series of misunderstandings, was one of my favorites. The complicated misunderstanding and interplay between Darcy and Bennet fascinated me.

I've always considered myself a romantic. That's probably why I'm still single. But I truly believe in old-fashioned romance. I just can't help it.

Instead, we have these dreadful dating apps like Splinter. I guess it's a great idea to use the internet to help singles meet on the web, but a lot about them bothered me. Unfortunately, in this century, the only way to meet people and find love, it seems, is to play the game.

It'd be nice if Splinter simply announced who 'LIKED' you as soon as that person swiped right. But instead, the app draws out the suspense and keeps its users flipping endlessly through profiles, wondering if each new face was *the one*.

Dutifully, I swiped to see who had 'LIKED' me.

My fingertips flipped through a stack of women's photos. I passed the usual drivel of ladies' room selfies (a weird place to hold a photoshoot, I think), salacious bikini shots, and photo filters with ultra-smoothed skin, digital puppy ears, and bug-eyed distortions with haste.

But then I stumbled on this one woman's page.

And stopped.

She was different. Her name was Corbin. She was twenty-eight, two years older than me. She wore her beauty casually. A silver nose ring hung from her nostril and a tattoo covered her freckled left arm. Every picture showed her doing something outdoorsy—wearing a pack on a narrow alpine pass. Wading near a waterfall. Giggling as an elephant trunk tickled her face.

I sat up straighter and blotted my palms which had suddenly

gone sweaty. *Finally*. This lady showed some personality. Her profile didn't scream, 'I'm lonely and have no photos to offer except car-selfies with digital puppy-snout filters.'

No, there was a real person here. For once.

Intrigued, I read her short bio. It didn't say much, leaving me with more questions than answers. I wondered: why don't people ever write more about themselves? It'd make the whole chatting-with-a-stranger-thing easier, that is, if we ever matched.

Oh man, I hoped so. I admired this woman who confidently displayed her real self to the world. And, judging from her pictures, Corbin resembled the kind of person I longed to date.

I swiped right, wondering if she might be my ticket off this dreadfully unromantic dating app. Forever.

———

CORBIN

I tossed my phone aside and decided to make lunch to take my mind off Splinter.

As I scrambled up some eggs, I told myself, don't get your hopes up. You'll probably never meet even Mohammed. Or any tolerable guy, for that matter. The nice ones always disappear. They evaporate into the ether. They're all too shy to make a move, leaving only the narcissist losers and their stupid gawping fish.

No, I'd probably end up an old spinster, surrounded by screeching green parakeets—

My phone *swooped*, interrupting my brooding. I grabbed for it. A notification from Splinter. My heart pounded. My index finger trembled as I opened the app.

Was it him? Did we match?

The confetti that burst on the screen matched my mood when Mohammed's pic filled the screen.

"IT'S A MATCH," the app's auto text announced. "GO MAKE A MOVE!"

Tingles flooded my whole system. My stomach flip-flopped and my hands shook as my toes clenched in my favorite pink-striped socks. I could not suppress a grin.

I opened the chat and found a tiny speech bubble already blinking at me.

Mohammed had started writing! But what would he say?

The longest ten minutes of my life dragged by as he wrote, paused, started again, and deleted what he'd written. He did that at least eight more times.

I wondered if my pounding heart would burst from waiting.

"Just send it already," I urged at the phone, knowing he couldn't hear. "Come on already!"

I shifted position. I couldn't stand still. I trembled, wondering what this guy would say.

At last, a message appeared with another *swoop*. It read, "I can see you have a lovely soul. And it clearly matches with your face."

"Aww, what a sweet thing to say," I said aloud.

I almost replied to him immediately. But then I caught myself. No, I couldn't do that. It'd make me seem too eager. And that's when guys lost interest. It happened to me before with this guy I'd matched with named Blaine.

I'd replied straight-away to his first texts and, not long after, he ghosted me. My last text had asked, "Why'd you disappear?"

And his reply (three days later) read, "BC ur 2 needy."

That was it. So, wanting a man who could hold a conversation made me needy, huh?

Well, I wouldn't lose Mohammed the same way. Instead, I left the Splinter chat open on my table. I ate my lunch and feigned disinterest. I'd reply eventually.

Besides, I had to get ready for work soon.

———

MOHAMMED

After sending my message and receiving only silence, cold uncertainty coursed through my veins. Would Corbin ever respond? Had I said too much and scared her off? God, what must she think of me?

This was the part of dating apps I hated. The waiting. The overanalyzing. Not knowing how a woman would interpret my message. I dislike the feeling of vulnerability, waiting on tenterhooks for someone else's validation. I hated revealing the squishy underbelly of my emotions, wondering if a prospective date will kick me there.

The bad ones usually do.

Another hour and a half dragged past before my phone vibrated.

Hastily, I scooped it up and read Corbin's reply.

"Thanx," she wrote. "U seem cool too."

That was it. Not exactly a promising start. I frowned.

However, I didn't want her to think I was just another player or that I wasn't interested in her so I sent back, "Is that really your best opening line?"

I followed this with a funny-faced emoji so she'd know I was joking and I added, "What's your favorite local place to eat?"

Sent.

Yes, it was cheesy, but what else was I supposed to say? It's always awkward messaging a stranger. I had no clue what she was into except for her tiny bio and a handful of pictures. I didn't know what tickled her sense of humor or her interests.

My stomach flip-flopped. I paced my bedroom, cracked my knuckles, and picked up a fidget-spinner, flicking it so hard it nearly broke. I replaced it on the shelf and checked my phone.

Still nothing.

I refreshed the app and waited. More precious minutes passed. Anxiety whispered at the back of my mind. Why hadn't she replied? Had I said something wrong? Had my last question been *too* personal? Too sappy? *What?*

I glanced at my phone a hundred times over the next two hours.

Guess, she wasn't interested after all. The initial high of matching with someone began to fade. Slowly, my worry shifted to murky disappointment.

I changed into exercise clothes, figuring I'd work out my frustration playing b-ball at the rec center.

———

CORBIN

I noticed the second message from Mohammed, with his teasing line and the funny emoji face. And then that third one about a restaurant. OMG, how obvious was that? But in, you know, an adorable kind of way. I knew exactly where *that* line of inquiry headed.

God, how I longed to answer him and express interest so he'd ask me out.

However, memories of Blaine, my past ghoster, haunted me. So instead of answering Mohammed's question, I drove to my job at the San Francisco Zoo—a forty-minute commute. Once I arrived, I clocked in and started my tasks with the animals—ensuring they were fed.

I had no interest in appearing 'needy' again. No, thank you.

A couple of hours passed before I had a free moment to send a message.

When I finally answered, I wrote, "Ethiopian food," adding a winky face so Mohammed would know that I understood his hint about a place to eat.

I pressed send and waited.

Giddy, I expected his next reply to come flying in at warp speed as all his others had. I couldn't wait for him to ask me out to dinner. Of course, I'd say yes.

Just not right away.

But my phone remained silent. No *swoop* indicated activity from

Splinter. Nor anything from Mohammed. It stayed quiet. Just like it did with Blaine…

Oh, no. Not again!

I waited a couple more hours, until my break. When Mohammed still hadn't replied, I risked appearing needy and playfully called him out. "What's the hold-up, big guy? Why no reply? Cat got your tongue?"

This time, my phone chimed an instant later. "Thought you weren't interested," he wrote.

I snorted and typed back. "Now why would you think that?"

"Because your replies took so long," he wrote. "And because they were so short. Texts like that shows me disinterest."

I read it through twice in surprise. He had a point. That's precisely what I did and it backfired.

"Sorry if I gave the wrong impression. I didn't want to seem too eager," I sent.

A long minute passed. Had I lost him with my charade of indifference? God, why couldn't dating be easier? How's a girl supposed to act when every man has such disparate communication styles?

I pushed my half-eaten snack aside. My appetite, like my earlier excitement, had fled.

Several minutes passed. I wondered what, if anything, he'd say.

At last, another message arrived. *Swoop!*

"I understand that," Mohammed said. "However, I need to be upfront here. I prefer straightforwardness in future communication if that's okay. I find playing games exhausting."

As I read the text, I shivered. Ooh! Here was a man who didn't mind being upfront about his communication preferences? Despite my reserve, it made me more interested by the minute. A distracting warmth spread through my belly.

My phone *swooped* again. I raced to open Mohammed's note.

He asked, "Having said that, would you wanna meet up and get some Ethiopian food tonight? As a first date?"

I beamed. All my insides lit up. Honestly, there's something magic about a man asking you to have dinner with him. It never got old. It's *almost* better than an orgasm.

"Yeah," I said. "I'd love to!"

"Really?" Mohammed asked. "When I've asked to meet up IRL, that's when people lose interest."

Boy, could I ever relate to that!

"No, I'd love to go," I texted. "It's usually guys who never want to meet up with me!"

"Well, their loss," he texted. "I'd rather meet someone like you IRL, than waste time messaging. See you tonight?"

"Yup! Looking forward to it."

As I put my phone down, my heart beat, pumping excitement through my veins. The idea of dining with Mohammed made me want to dress up and look my best. He hadn't made me feel badly about myself as Blaine had done. Instead, I found Mohammed's directness attractive and more than a little arousing.

I knew I was expecting a lot from someone I'd never met, but I had a good feeling, an intuition about him and his character, something I hadn't found with other dates, or on the other men's profiles.

I sensed this guy could be one of the good ones.

Euphoria flooded through me and I allowed all the fuzzy feels to embrace me like a comfy sweater. For once, instead of worrying, I began to wonder.

Could this be my last first date ever? Had that miserable app finally succeeded in matching us? Could it be that Mohammed and I had finally won the endless swiping game? And in doing so, had we hit the jackpot?

I nibbled at my lip.

Something told me it might be so.

DATING IN COVID

SKYE BALLANTYNE

Classical music danced through the open doors. Liviana took a step forward, her heart in her soles. Jessamy took Liviana's hand with a nod of her head. Jessamy had to convince Liviana to come with her. She had pled and begged for weeks before Liviana had finally relented and agreed to come, on the condition that Jessamy had to make sure she had appropriate attire for the event, and man did Jessamy come through. They were both dressed to the nines in dresses that would be the envy of any ballroom dance.

If Liviana was being honest, she felt a little ridiculous all dressed up the way she was. She was a simple girl who very rarely dressed up and even more rarely did her hair and makeup, especially not in the fancy way that she had on now. Liviana wrinkled her nose slightly as the mere thought of her makeup made her face itch. She didn't want to risk scratching it and smudging all the hard work Jessamy had put into making her so beautiful.

Jessamy took Livana's hand and the two of them walked down the stairs and onto the ballroom floor. By the time they had reached the last step, the dance had ended, leaving people mingling about, trying to figure out who their next dance partner was going to be for the evening. Jessamy, naturally, was swept up the moment her feet hit the last step, leaving Liviana on her own.

Liviana began to edge her way toward the refreshment table, her normal hang out for events that she didn't quite feel comfortable at. If she had to be uncomfortable and feel awkward, the least she could do was eat. That was supposed to take her mind off of how much she wanted to bolt for the door, and it did, for the most part. Food was a good wing person, and never asked too much of you.

It wasn't that Liviana didn't like going out, she did. And it wasn't even a matter of simply not liking dancing, because she did. In fact, she loved dancing. She just didn't do well with people. She didn't know what to do when she got thrown into a crowded room, or in a room full of people she didn't know. Her lungs would start to contract, cutting off her air supply, and she would feel her limbs begin to shake uncontrollably as a pit would begin to form in the bottom of her stomach, and a chill would settle in on her. No matter how many layers she wore, she would still be able to feel the chill, and wouldn't be able to stop the shaking.

"May I have this dance?" a raven masked man with sandy brown hair asked, holding out his hand to her.

She stared at him. Her eyes widened in surprise. She hadn't expected to be asked to dance the first dance after coming into the ballroom. It usually took her twenty dances to be seen by a man, and then a few more dances before he finally decided to take pity on her and ask her to dance. Never before had she been asked to dance so quickly.

"Come on," the man begged, "Dance with me," he asked, his eyes widening, giving the look of a puppy dog.

Liviana tried to glance down at her dress, but he wouldn't allow her gaze to leave his face. It was as if he knew the power his look held, and he knew that it would lose all that power if she looked away from him. He wasn't going to let that happen.

"Come on, you can pretend the world doesn't exist," he

suggested, his eyebrows rising as a smile played on his face, "You can pretend that I'm Mr. Darcy, coming to sweep you off your feet."

"Well, if you're Mr. Darcy then I wouldn't be dancing with you. I would throw this punch in your face and then well, I probably would actually punch your face, just for good measure," she laughed.

"Wow," the man laughed, "Not an Austen fan, that's fine, we can still dance and pretend we're somewhere else. It's New Year's Eve, the time to indulge in fantasy."

"Oh, I'm a huge Austen fan," Liviana countered, she had read all of Jane Austen's books and had watched several of the adaptations. She loved getting carried away into the story of Mansfield Park, or Persuasion, especially Persuasion. She didn't know how anyone couldn't love Persuasion. It was by far Jane Austen's best book, "I'm just not a Darcy fan. I think he's an arrogant, self-righteous pig of a man and Jane Austen should have had him killed off, preferably in a horrible carriage accident with Elizabeth Bennett."

"Got it," the man said, "Well then, I'm not Mr. Darcy, I am..." he paused for a moment as he tried to come up with another Austen hero.

"Pick one," she said, "Any of them are better than Mr. Darcy, even the villains of the story would be a better choice than Mr. Darcy."

"Well," he said, "Then why don't you pretend that I am, Captain Frederick Wentworth, at your service?" he bowed deeply, thankful that his sister had just forced him to watch Persuasion, giving him the perfect name to choose.

Liviana's heart leaped inside her chest. Of all the Austen men he could have chosen, he had certainly chosen the best one of the bunch. With a choice like that, she figured she could overlook the whole Darcy fiasco of their first introduction. Liviana reached her hand out to his and he led her onto the dance floor.

Liviana stared into the face of the man who was calling himself Captain Frederick Wentworth as they glided across the dance floor. She could almost believe that he really was the man of Austen's novel. She had taken his hand and danced with him and her reality disappeared. There was no going back.

Liviana felt her heart drop when the dance ended and Wentworth escorted her off of the dance floor. He took her hand and bowed over it, thankfully, without the kiss. It was as if he somehow knew that since she didn't like Darcy, a hand kiss would be a no-go as well. Or maybe he thought that a kiss on the hand was just as weird and creepy as Liviana did. Whatever the reason, she was glad he had forgone the kiss.

"May I have this dance?" another man asked, stepping in and ready to take Liviana off of Wentworth's hand for the next dance.

Liviana glanced over at Wentworth. She had hoped that he would ask her to dance again. The look on his face told her a different story, however. He simply stood aside, allowing the stranger to lead Liviana out onto the dance floor.

He wasn't nearly as graceful a dancer as Wentworth was. There was no way she could escape reality when he was dancing with her. He was too rigid, too uncomfortable in his movements. Although, to his credit, he knew the steps a lot better than Wentworth had. But his dance was mechanical, practical, and passionless. Liviana's eyes kept glancing around, wondering where Wentworth was in the crowd, hoping that he would be close enough after the dance ended that they would be able to pair up. Alas, that wasn't to be.

Dance after dance, she found herself too far away from Wentworth to be swooped up into another dance with him. Instead, she danced with the rest of the men until her feet began to swell and she couldn't breathe. Exhausted, she slumped into a chair that had been provided and watched as the dancers began yet another dance.

"You look like you could use some company," a man said, sitting down beside her.

She recognized him as one of the men she had danced with previously. He had made her skin crawl just by looking at her. She couldn't place the reason why. He seemed as if he was a nice enough fellow, and he didn't look dirty by any means, but the mere look of him made Liviana want to go take the longest, hottest shower she could.

"No," Liviana said, "I just want to sit here quietly. No company required."

"Oh come on, you and I both know that when a girl says no they never actually mean no. It's just a way to tell a guy to try harder."

Liviana wanted to deck him right then and there. What kind of old-timey idiocy was that? She couldn't believe the sheer stupidity of what he had just said.

"No," Liviana said, "It doesn't. No means no, or in the cases that it doesn't, it means get the hell away from me right now."

Liviana's eyes darted around the room hoping to find Jessamy somewhere in the dancers, hoping to be able to catch her eye and beg her for help, but Jessamy was lost in a sea of dancers. Liviana would just have to deal with this alone.

"Oh, you're a feisty one. I like that in a girl," he smiled, and Liviana's skin crawled.

She wondered if she would ever feel clean again after this conversation. She somehow doubted it.

"What do you say we take this outside?" he continued to smile at her, giving her a look that even Liviana, in all her naive glory, meant that he was thinking they were going to do more than have a conversation about what is really meant when a girl says no.

"No," Liviana said again, "You can go outside, but I'm going to stay inside."

"Oh come on," the man persisted, "You know you won't be able to resist me for long. Women never can."

He grabbed at her hand and tried to pull her to her feet. Liviana struggled to get her hand back, but his grip was too firm. Liviana began to shake as a fear she had never before felt washed over her. She had never been one of those women who always carried mace in their purse, and didn't walk alone after dark. Unlike most women, she had been lucky enough to feel safe in her world. She never took the precautions that so many other women did in order to keep themselves, and had never had the fear to motivate those precautions, until that moment.

Suddenly, it came crashing down on her and it felt like she had been rammed by a semi. The world was a dangerous place, a scary place, especially for a woman. Liviana was hit by the fear that so many women felt. The fear of what this man would do, the fear of not knowing what this man was capable of. He could kill her if he wanted to. She was an easy target.

He had at least 100 pounds on her. She had no training in self-defense, she had no mace to spray him with, she didn't even have so much as a key that she could use as a weapon to fight him off with. He could do whatever he wanted with her, and there was nothing she could do to stop it. She tried to scream, to alert someone, anyone of what was going on, but she found that the fear had blocked off her voice.

"Why don't you let her go?" Liviana recognized the voice and a flood of relief washed over her, temporarily overcoming the fear.

"Why don't you butt out of this?" the man snarled, refusing to let go of her hand.

"She said she didn't want to go outside with you, so why don't you listen to her wishes and leave her alone?"

"She doesn't know what she wants. Not until I show her."

"I think you better leave," Wentworth said, Liviana could see his hands beginning to curl into a fist.

The man snarled at Wentworth, but with his deeds brought to light and a scene about to be made, he stormed off.

"Are you alright?" Wentworth asked as the man left the ballroom.

Liviana's limbs had turned to jelly, and if she hadn't been sitting down at that moment, she surely would have fallen onto the chair. She was still shaking uncontrollably and there was a vice around her lungs, making it difficult for her to draw in an actual breath of air. Tears began to prick her eyes, but she held them off.

"Did he hurt you?" Wentworth asked, kneeling down in front of her.

He kept his hands to himself as he looked at her, his eyes full of compassion and worry about what her answer was going to be.

Liviana shook her head. She didn't trust herself to speak. If she opened her mouth, the tears would take that as a reason to start streaming down her face, and if there was anything that she didn't want, it was to start crying.

"Can I get you something?" Wentworth asked, "Water? A cookie?"

The thought of Wentworth leaving her alone caused all that fear to rise up inside of her again and she could feel herself beginning to hyperventilate.

"Hey, it's okay," Wentworth said, he reached out his hand and Liviana grasped it in a death grip, "Just take some deep breaths for me."

Liviana tried to, but she was finding it difficult to take in enough air to get a full deep breath. With the hand that wasn't in Liviana's death grip, Wentworth removed his mask.

"Can you tell me your name?" Wentworth asked, trying a different tactic.

"Liv.....liv..." Liviana gasped, "Liviana," she hadn't realized that her name was such a difficult one until that moment.

"It's nice to meet you Liviana," Wentworth smiled, "My name is Alec."

Liviana nodded. She had preferred Frederick Wentworth, but she guessed she could make do with Alec.

"Hey, Liviana," Alec continued, "Can you tell me five things you can see?"

Liviana looked around her, "Um... a raven mask," she said, her eyes falling on the mask Alec had taken off his face, "My dress, your hair, the dancers, and um, the chair."

"Good," Alec encouraged, "That was really good," he moved

himself so that he was sitting in a more comfortable position, "How about four things you can touch?"

"Um," Liviana said, all of a sudden everything she could feel disappeared from memory, "My dress," she finally said, playing with the satin fabric in her hand, "My mask," suddenly the mask felt too tight against her face. Although it didn't cover her mouth, she felt as if it was suffocating her. With her free hand, she ripped it off of her face, "The chair, your hand," she hadn't realized how warm his hand was until that moment.

Liviana and Alec both looked down at their hands. Liviana's was white as it gripped Alec's hand tightly. Noticing how tightly she was holding his hand, Liviana relaxed her hold ever so slightly allowing blood to once again flow through Alec's hand.

"You're doing great," Alec encouraged, "Now, three things you can hear."

Liviana was starting to feel calmer as she said, "The dresses rustling," she smiled as a dancer danced past them, "The band," she thought, straining her hearing, "You," she finally said, when nothing else came to mind.

"How about smell? What are two things you can smell?"

"The cookies," they smelled heavenly, freshly out of the oven. She took another deep breath, "You," his cologne wafted toward her nose. There was something comforting about that smell.

"Last one. What is one thing you can taste?"

"Those cookies," Liviana smiled.

Now that she had smelled them she wanted nothing more than to eat one.

Alec laughed, "Would you like me to get you a cookie?"

Liviana nodded, and Alec gently untangled his hand from hers and went to retrieve the cookie.

"I heard what had happened," Jessamy said, rushing over to Liviana's side, "Are you alright?"

"I'm fine," Liviana said. Alec had done well in talking her down, but she also found that she wasn't really in a party mood any longer, "I'm just tired. Can we go home?"

Jessamy's face fell, "I guess," she said. She had wanted to stay at least until midnight. It was New Year's Eve after all. She had wanted to ring in the year 2020 at the dance, not at home on the couch, but after what Liviana had just been through, Jessamy couldn't deny her the right to go home.

"I can take her," Alec said, presenting Liviana with her coveted cookie, "If you want," he hurried to add.

He had had enough of the dance as well and wanted to make sure Liviana got home safely. Jessamy looked hopefully toward Liviana. Her eyes begged to let Alec's offer be alright. Liviana nodded. That was acceptable to her. Jessamy hugged her friend and hurried off to another dance while Alec and Liviana made their way to Liviana's apartment.

Alec had just escorted Liviana up the steps to her door when fireworks started going off around them. Alec glanced down at his watch. It was midnight. The new year had officially begun.

"Happy New Year, Anne," Alec bowed low.

"Happy New Year, Frederick," Liviana smiled.

With a kiss to ring in the new year, Liviana and Alec parted ways, never, in their wildest moments thinking that they would ever see each other again. However, neither one of them could have expected what would happen next.

A few months later a lockdown was announced, and people were told to stay inside and refrain from getting together. Schools closed. Liviana lost her job. And Jessamy was struggling to cover the full rent on her reduced hours due to the pandemic.

One day, Liviana and Jessamy decided it was time to brave the stores. They were out of everything, and had started having to use leaves for toilet paper, and steal the crumbs from the ants for food.

The grocery store was completely empty. The shelves were bare. Liviana wouldn't have been at all surprised to see a tumbleweed roll on past.

"Hey look," Jessamy laughed, holding up a can of baby corn, "I guess no one ever really likes baby corn, do they?"

It was the only thing left on the shelves. So, it looked like they would be eating baby corn for a while. Liviana tried to follow Jessamy's example and laugh and try to look on the bright side of things, but it did nothing to shine a light on the ever-darkening fear that she was feeling inside.

"I'm going to go find some toilet paper," Liviana said.

"Good luck," Jessamy said, "You'll need it."

As luck would have it, she managed to find a four-pack of single-ply toilet paper. It would have to work. It was the only one left. She could feel someone else grabbing it at the same time.

"Hey," Liviana said, trying to take it back.

"Want to go halfsies?" the man said.

Liviana looked over. It was Wentworth. Her heart started beating rapidly in her chest and she forgot how to speak, although that could have been because she had been locked in her house for several months.

"Yeah," Liviana finally said.

They could make do with two rolls. They'd have to. They'd figure something out.

"You know," Alec said, "When we left I kept kicking myself for not getting your number, and I promised myself that if I ever saw you again, I would get your number. So, can I have your number?"

Liviana laughed and gave him her number. For one single moment, there was a bit of light at the never-ending tunnel.

The promise of tomorrow, the promise of an end in sight began to hang over people's heads, and Liviana couldn't help but feel the excitement that the end was near.

'What will you do when this is all over?' Liviana texted Alec one night.

'I don't really know,' Alec texted back.

'Well, what do you want to do?'

'I want....' he paused as he ran his fingers through his hair, not sure if he should type his response. He wasn't sure that Liviana was ready for him to say what he wanted, 'Never mind what I want. What do you want?' he finally finished his text and sent it.

'That's not gonna fly,' Liviana texted back, 'I won't tell you what I want until you tell me what you want.'

'You. Always you.'

His thumbs hovered over the send button. They twitched, ready to send it, ready to deliver it to her, to tell her his true feelings once and for all. His thumbs wanted to send the message out into the universe, just to see what he got back. Just as he was about to send it, he found himself chickening out and erasing the whole message.

'I want another dance,' he typed, 'With you.'

He quickly pushed the send button before he could chicken out once again. His stomach dropped as it went through. Some part of him had been hoping that it would fail to send the message. Some part of him had wished that he could bring it back and change his answer, but the universe had other plans. It wanted to see where this would go, where this would lead, and so it happily sent the message right on through, without a care to the man who was in anguish over having sent it.

Liviana read the message, her heart tingling. She loved dancing with him and she was glad that he obviously felt the same way, at least enough to want to dance with her again when all of this was over. If it was ever over.

One minute it would seem as if the end was in sight. They had an end-day in sight. Then, as quickly as they could see the light at the end of the tunnel, it would darken again, as the end date was once again moved.

'I'd like that too,' Liviana responded.

Breath returned to Alec's body as he read the message. He hadn't ruined anything with his message. He hadn't scared her too badly. His heart soared and he began to daydream about the day when they would get another dance.

TWIN
LEIGH ALDER

"Gemma! Over here!" I raised my hand slightly and waved. A few of the regulars turned in their seats and followed my gaze.

She wound through the uncharacteristically empty bar, plopped her purse on the table, and slid into the chair opposite me. Early afternoon on a Tuesday; the tables hadn't even had time to acquire their daily dose of sloshed beer and sticky ketchup.

"When you said the intersection of 12th and 4th, I thought you'd lost your mind."

I called her a New York neophyte, and signaled our server; she grinned and glided from behind the bar. Gemma asked what I had in front of me. Our server answered, a dirty martini. The drink had become my standard at my favorite watering hole; all the servers and bartenders handed me a glass before I could open my mouth.

Gemma turned up her nose and smiled, "Make mine a Manhattan." She turned to me, "When in Rome." She spun the bar napkin the server left and leaned in. "So, do you come here often?" I nodded. "At two o'clock?"

I laughed out loud and shook my head. "But if you want a table and the chance to hear someone talking to you, sooner rather than later is the rule for this place."

This place, one of the last lesbian bars in Manhattan, sat on a corner in the West Village, near the Stonewall Inn. At just a few hundred feet, everything was tight at the Snug, not just the drinks. Even the décor crowded upon itself. Still decked for St. Patrick's Day, paper shamrocks, pots of gold, and leprechauns jumbled in with green crepe fronds and grasses, all dangling from the ceiling. It looked like an Emerald Isle explosion.

Opposite our table, a walnut bar ran the length of the room, broken only by points of access for servers and pourers. Stools clustered along, some sitting side by side and others grouped by last night's patrons; no one bothered to regiment their placement; tonight's crowd would just move them again. Sunlight poured into the windows next to our table and through the entire corner of the building facing 12th Street and sidling along 4th Avenue.

Our server returned with Gemma's drink and we clinked glasses. "To old friends," she said and I echoed. I smiled as she sipped her drink and looked around the bar. Gemma had been my best friend and study buddy at Stanford Law. She and I stayed in touch even after we settled in far-flung cities to pursue our careers. Me to New York and her to Chicago. She was one of only five people I invited to my wedding; at her wedding, I wore the dress she chose and stood as her Maid of Honor.

A year later she called me late one night crying and telling me her marriage to Nate Sidwell imploded; he'd been cheating since their honeymoon. I told her to pack, freeze her accounts, and get to New York on the next plane. We coordinated, and I met her in baggage claim. She'd paid a lot of money to fly all those suitcases here, so I snagged the last luggage cart and piled it high.

We went to the apartment I shared with my wife, and I fed her tea and chicken soup and chocolate. She had all she could do to stay hydrated and eat a little something every day. But a week later, she bounced onto her feet, landed a job and put in a bid on her own place. I drew up her divorce papers and overnighted them to her old Chicago firm for immediate filing; we needed to work fast to keep her assets out of Nate's underemployed hands. Meanwhile, she deleted every picture of him except one from their wedding. She said she wanted a reminder not to make the same mistake twice.

Now, I told her she'd need to file those same papers for me. Fast. She took a deep breath. "When you took in your waif from the airport, you two seemed so...happy." She stopped talking and studied the streetscape. "No. That's not it. You weren't happy; you were settled." She faced me, "Settled." Pursing her lips, "What went wrong?"

After mulling her question for a minute, I told her about a typical evening a few nights before she moved to New York. In a fit to polish my knowledge of the classics, I'd pulled Plato's *Symposium* off the shelf and reread it. The Ancient Greek's worldview fascinated me, especially his improbable ideas about human longing. But, that's where the evening became a headache-inducing well of empty. I set the scene for Gemma.

"A Typical Evening at Home"

Scene: An elegant, not quite homey, American living room in an upscale Manhattan apartment. Couches and chairs are expensive and coordinated without predictably matching. Tasteful, original artwork adorns the walls. The television plays in the background, but no one pays attention to it. Me has started reading a new novel, <u>Turning a Page</u>. Wife is glued to her cell phone.

Me: This book reminds me of *Symposium*. You know? Plato's work *Symposium*.

Wife: Hmm?

Me: Yeah. Plato postulates that in some pre-conscious state, we're all round beings with one side ourselves and the other side our perfect mate.

Wife: Huh.

Me: Only we're back-to-back, so we can't see our other half.

Wife: (*continues to focus on her phone*)

Me: So, we're all terribly frustrated because we can't see, or touch, or kiss our perfect match, our twin.

Wife: We didn't have enough people at work again today. Paul and Julie both called out. I had five extra clients! Five! It sucks. It's not fair.

Me: (*sighs*) Sorry to hear you had a bad day again. Never mind.

Wife: (*defensive and irritated*) I'm listening.

Me: (*knows Wife's not listening, sounds rote*) So, we're connected to and separated from our other, our twin, all at the same time. Until the gods split us into two beings and we're born individually. That's why we spend our lives looking for 'the one.' We're seeking our twin. Some search female to male, some female to female, and some male to male. (*after a pause*) Anyway, this novel has those same themes.

Wife: (*sends phone to Me's face like a projectile*) Aww. Look. Beth got a new puppy.

Me: Great. Very cute.

(*Both go back to their own amusements before the interruption of interaction.*)

"The blandness wore me out." I leaned back.

Gemma rested her arm on the table and insisted that she hadn't seen any trouble brewing when she stayed with us. I gave her a refresher course on hostess manners and reminded her of her own Nate Sidwell-induced turmoil at the time. She nodded, reluctantly remembering.

"So, you're jumping ship." Gemma drained her Manhattan and our server appeared at our table with an expectant look. Gemma covered her glass and ordered a sparkling water.

"Lightweight," I teased but ordered the same for myself. I felt sure we'd get back to the hard stuff as the afternoon went on.

"You're still wearing your ring." She narrowed her eyes at me and sucked on the end of her drink sword.

"I promised to keep it on until the divorce is final. That's one reason why I need you to file the papers post-haste."

She asked why I'd made such a commitment when I was breaking the primary one, and I mumbled some gibberish about guilt, without feeling guilty in the least. I confessed to taking it off when it might be inconvenient to show a wedding band.

"You're already looking then?"

"I've already found."

Gemma's eyes lit like a roaring fire at Christmas. "So, that's why you've been scarce these last couple of months." She ogled me and leaned well across the table. "Let's hear it. Start from the beginning and leave out *no* details."

I told her about Jon Bateman, a senior partner at my firm with an inordinately large head to match his ego. He'd pawned a client off on me for a case he considered beneath him. A simple matter of an investment firm to the stars that finally got caught with its grubby hands in the till. The IRS sniffed them out by sending large tax bills and threatening letters to several high-profile people. Then they leaked the story to the media, and the negative publicity had the rich and famous up in arms.

Bateman's client was one of those people. He laid out the basics of the case and gave me the codes for her files and informed me I'd now be representing Eliza Doolittle.

"*Eliza Doolittle?*" Gemma cackled the code name a little too loudly. Several heads turned. She covered her tracks by catching the eye of our server and signaling two more drinks for our table.

"Okay. So Eliza Doolittle's coming in," She wiped a couple of tears from her eyes.

I told her how I'd prepared by reading Ms. Doolittle's entire folder, from birth certificate to last will and testament. I didn't need all that, but I'd been curious and read it anyway. I sent my clerk off researching precedents and told my secretary to hold all calls except client emergencies. She asked about calls from my wife; I told her to hold those especially. She raised an eyebrow, but she's discreet and didn't make any comment. On the way home the day before my meeting, I stopped in Alexander's on Fifth Avenue and bought a new outfit, a loose-tailored navy pinstripe suit with a primary-color-block fitted blouse.

Gemma raised an eyebrow at me as our server appeared with round two. She laid out fresh napkins and placed our drinks. She took the old glasses and Gemma's sword away.

Bateman came back in on the morning of and tried to act nonchalant but quizzed me about the case. He twisted around my office, picking up and putting down folders and pens and a picture of Diane. I growled at him, accused him of second-guessing his own junior partner, of dismissing women lawyers, and of poor taste in suits. He left saying Eliza'd be uncomfortable in the conference room I'd booked; she preferred smaller spaces.

"So when the front desk buzzed, I extracted her from her entourage and brought her back to my office." I sat back and took a sip, letting Gemma take it all in and draw some conclusions.

"You're not dating a client. Tell me you're not dating a client." Gemma paused with her glass in midair. "Diane'll have every penny you've got, just to keep that quiet."

"Give me some credit." I ate one of the five olives our server had speared for me; I like my martinis really dirty.

Gemma wound up, "So what, you've taken up with her hair designer? Make-up artist? A bodyguard?" She took a swig.

"No. I've given her file back to Bateman." I sat up straight, "I'm allowed to date the firm's clients who aren't mine."

"That's a thin area and getting thinner all the time." Gemma's eyes darted around. I could tell she wanted to line up drink three; I'd given her something serious to worry about with my divorce.

"I followed ethics guidelines at the time of occurrence. When she was my client, we weren't dating. When we began dating, she was no longer my client." Our server appeared and I asked for two more. She raised an eyebrow at me but nodded. I smiled and, as a show of good faith, took a gulp of the water still sitting in front of me.

Gemma finished her drink and exhaled long and slow, "Okaaay. Go on."

At our first meeting, I dispensed with the legal matters in thirty minutes. I'd done that much advance work and secured that many commitments. I just needed her to sign a few papers for my secretary to notarize. When she didn't get up to leave, I asked if she had any more questions. She asked if I knew only two percent of the world's population had green eyes. Hers sent fireworks shooting into mine.

Gemma slapped the table and laughed, "What a pick-up line."

She came into the office every day that week. By Friday, I knew I'd have to give her legal file back to Bateman. I explained why to her; she reached over, squeezed my fingers and whispered, "Finally." We made a date for the following Wednesday afternoon, the next time she'd be in town. I met her at the AM Elixir around the corner from my office; it's even pricier than the ones in Uptown and Brooklyn.

Gemma whistled, "You can afford that place?" She still worried about the divorce settlement.

"Only just. But, Eliza can."

"Don't you think it's about time you told me who *Eliza* is?"

"Attorney-client privilege?" I assaulted my napkin, tearing a fringe along one side.

"Best friend privilege." Gemma smiled into my eyes, "It goes deeper."

I glanced toward the narrow aisle between us and the slowly filling bar stools; I whispered, "Sophia George."

Gemma's mouth dropped. She forgot to breathe. Of course, she knew the name; practically everyone on the planet knows her name. Her first big feature film came at the advanced age of twelve, and twenty-some years later, she's more in demand than ever.

I continued my story. At first, we met at her place every time she came through town; we danced together; we told stories; we watched favorite movies. She bought me a cupcake for my birthday.

Gemma rested her forehead in her hand. She pitied me. I knew I sounded pathetic, but I didn't take anything back. "So you hole up in her apartment like a couple of romance refugees?"

"Not entirely." We'd learned how to get around. I figured out why she couldn't be anonymous. It was her hair, her distinctive dark auburn hair. To be sure, she wore hats to cover it, and large dark glasses to cover her eyes, and looping scarves to obscure her singular profile. But still the hair. The solution? Lose the hat; wear a hood. We tried it one afternoon. It worked. And it opened a world of possibilities. We roamed, freed.

We went into the Park and around the reservoir, through Village shops, to museums. We walked along the river by the docks and gazed over the water, watching the boats come and go; she leaned against me and my arms wrapped around her. No one recognized her.

"And that's enough for you?" Gemma squinted at me. "You've thrown over your marriage for wandering around town with a woman wearing a hoodie?"

"I told you what my marriage was like." My tone came out too sharp, "Sorry."

I paused. "Listen. I shouldn't have gotten married in the first place, but at the time, it seemed like the next logical step. Financially sound, and all that." I curled my lip, "Not enough anymore."

"I know this is going to sound corny as hell, but it's like she's the yin to my yang and I'm the yin to hers." I drummed my fingers on the table and studied the beer taps like I'd never seen them before.

"Oh, my God." Gemma stopped moving and stared. "That's absolutely disgusting."

I set my jaw. Determined to explain what I meant and regain some dignity.

We each had an odd relationship with commitment. I love it; I married someone I shouldn't have, just so I'd have the permanence, the stability. She'll probably never marry. She protects her freedom with the bloodlust of a hunting eagle.

Sophia comes from a broken home. Silly euphemism for a family ripped apart. Her parents made all the usual vows, and then one by one her father broke them. He left before she could form sentences. Her scandalized Catholic grandparents gave her mother enough money for a one-way ticket from Ireland to Canada and told her to forget their names. The whole experience left her mother bankrupt and bitter. Still, she created a life for them. But it left Sophia feeling guilty. They made their own way to the States a few years later. She promised herself she'd never be in that position again; no one would do to her what her father did to her and her mother.

Our server came over; it had taken her a little longer to get back to us since the bar began filling up. I told Gemma she had to try their burger; it qualified as the after-life on a bun. She asked the server what made them so special and received an enigmatic smile in return. We ordered two with fries and a big bottle of ketchup. We felt it our evening's duty to smear the red stuff on our table.

I shifted in my seat and began the next part of my story. Gemma only knew part of my history: came out at age fifteen, paid my way through law school. But she didn't know about my childhood or my parents. Almost no one did. My parents stayed together. For my sake, they said. Really, I think they just liked the boxing practice; they hit each other, and they hit me. They spent a lot of time hitting me. A hobby of sorts. They did other things, too. I don't ever talk about that. It makes me angry and uncertain and vulnerable. And I don't like those feelings. I needed to escape the chaos and the violence, so I built myself a stable career, and I found it rewarding. I went into a stable marriage, and I found it hateful.

Our server appeared with two plates overflowing with grilled sirloin, melting cheese, and still-sizzling fries. Gemma gasped at the five-sense sensation placed before her. She plopped ketchup on her plate, some landing on the table, and proceeded to burn her mouth on a too-hot-to-handle sliver of golden tuber. She laughed at herself and bit into the sandwich. She made all the guttural noises of a woman in love.

About a third of the way through her dinner, she paused long enough to ask if I started sleeping with Sophia that first week. I assured her I hadn't; in fact, we'd shown admirable restraint in our clandestine-electric-chaste meetings. We took some time to get to know each other.

She smirked, "You're kidding, right? The two of you can't stay away from each other but you adhered to courtly love?"

"I didn't say that." I put some more ketchup on my plate and swirled a couple of fries in it. "We were more like two uncertain teenagers at the first school dance."

"This just keeps getting better," Gemma laughed and bit into her burger again.

"She had to get used to the idea of seeing a woman, and I had some quaint notions about the sanctity of marriage." I paused and watched a couple of young women, arms entwined, stumble through the door. "When it came right down to it, though, I threw all my quaint notions right out."

I hadn't cheated on Diane before, although I'd had opportunities. But the force field of Sophia couldn't be denied. So, I stopped trying. I paused my story, sat back and watched Gemma polish off her dinner. She didn't leave a scrap. Full of protein and carbs, she turned in her seat, looking for our server. She knew the story didn't end there, and she wanted another Manhattan.

Our server came by to clear our plates and take another drink order. Gemma got her cocktail, but I switched to sparkling water. Sophia was scheduled back in town late tonight or early tomorrow morning. Either way, I didn't want to sleep through her arrival because I'd had too much to drink.

Gemma narrowed her eyes at me, "You know, I'm not really surprised by this." She nodded her head like a hindsight soothsayer. "Your name just didn't work with Diane's. There's no poetry there," Gemma smiled up at our server who'd arrived with our drinks.

"What are you talking about?" I pined at the sight of her Manhattan; any other night I'd have had another martini. But, I envisioned Sophia and smiled over the rim of my water glass.

"Your names. They didn't seem like they belonged together. When you first told me about her, I figured she'd be another one of your short-term flings. I figured you'd come to your senses before it was too late." She blinked at me and watched the young couple, who now sat at the bar, kissing their way through their first beers.

"You didn't say anything." I frowned at her.

"And you didn't say anything when I married Nate the Narcissist." She drank some of her water, still sitting on the table from earlier in the afternoon.

She had me there. I hadn't liked Nate from the start. He spent too much time staring into mirrors and smoothing his hair. He also spent too much time looking at the breasts and butt of every woman who walked by. I knew he wouldn't be faithful; I just didn't know the extent.

"I mean, listen to her name. Diane. Di--ane. Paired with yours, there's no..." She rubbed her thumb and two fingers together. "There's no, 'je ne sais quoi'" She gazed at the sparkly shamrock dangling over our table. "Even printed on the wedding invitations, your names didn't look right, didn't look like they belonged side-by-side." She sat up straight and tipped her head back, eyes steady and unblinking: she gave me the look she'd give a jury after a brilliant closing argument.

"Now. Sophia. That works. It works so well you two could have been Victorian 'best friends' or you could be travelers from the future. Your names are timeless." Gemma drained her Manhattan and leaned into the table.

I pulled her glass away from her. "I'm cutting you off."

She snickered, "Okay, Mom." She looked around the packed bar at the patrons who'd come in since we first sat down. Older women leaning together and laughing, middle aged women griping about their jobs, girls flashing fake IDs and grinning at anyone who gave them the time of day. Gemma refocused on my story and smirked, "So when did you two finally move past chaste, and you know, do the deed?"

I rubbed my forehead with my thumb and forefinger.

"Don't play coy with me now. Get on with it."

I wondered, on a scale of one to ten, just how drunk she was and how much of this she'd remember in the morning. I gave her the sobriety test we used in law school when we'd been too long in a bar: summarize the Craig v. Boren case from Oklahoma and the 14th amendment argument Ginsburg used. An Oklahoma statute barred boys, like Craig, from purchasing low-alcohol beer before the age of twenty-one; girls, however, could purchase beer at age eighteen. Ginsburg argued that, because of gender, the state law did not provide equal protection to Craig and was therefore unconstitutional. Ginsburg won, and Gemma passed her test.

Sophia and I had been spending endless afternoons in her swish apartment, just eight blocks north of the one I shared with Diane. We'd spent a good percentage of those afternoons kissing before I finally lost my moral reservations and she lost her apprehensions.

She'd arranged for a week off between obligations and wanted to spend it with me. I mumbled something at Diane about a work trip, consulting on a case involving a big client and moving through the Boston courts. I gave her more information than I needed to. That should have been a tell. But, I knew she wouldn't question; she never questioned anything I did or didn't do. She never paid attention.

So, I packed a suitcase and showed up at Sophia's building. By that time the doorman knew me and let me in. I was giddy and had insisted on taking her out to Syncopate, and I wouldn't take no for an answer; I'd made reservations. We had a secluded table in a quiet corner; plants and partitions shielded us from view. I wanted her to myself, and she wanted me.

We shared a bottle of wine and ordered the Gulf prawns and Maine lobster. For dessert, handmade chocolates and a glass of chilled champagne. We dined in peace, but I took her there to dance, after all. She loves dancing as much as I do. On the floor, we went on full display. Everyone in the place could see us, but we only saw each other. So, I didn't notice Diane and her sisters sitting about twenty feet from the band. They didn't cause a scene, just abandoned their dinners and left. She used my card to pay; can't say I blame her.

"That's how she found out?" Gemma's eyes got big. "And you want me to preserve your assets in the divorce?"

I sat up straight and nodded.

"You know that's an undergraduate move, right? Showing off the new girlfriend right in front of the old." Gemma sucked on her latest drink sword, no doubt savoring the essence of Maker's Mark.

"It's not like I intended for it to happen. I didn't ask Sophia to a club where I knew Diane would be." I defended myself as badly as a middle school debate team. "I meant to tell her quietly, at home. Let her scream at me and throw things." I glanced out the window at the nighttime street. Diane kicked me out. Even though my money bought us that apartment, I didn't argue. I packed a few things and turned up at Sophia's door.

Gemma rested her head in her hand, "Go on. Not a play-by-play. But let's have something juicy to offset the blunder. What happened after you two left the club?"

I smiled. We'd been loud. We'd been frenzied. We'd been up all night. Paused for coffee in the morning. Repeat. Nothing more to say.

"Sounds idyllic," Gemma's eyes went misty.

I thought about her word. Idyllic. The stuff of every Rom Com ever made. Gazing deeply into each other's eyes. Holding hands in darkened restaurant corners. Dancing the night away. Cue the violins and rose petals. Except.

The little issue of her commitment-aversion and my commitment-craving. Gemma stopped worrying her napkin, pitying me again.

I wiggled my wedding ring off my finger and laid it on the table. I held out my right hand and showed her another ring. Small and gold with a diamond chip. The birthstone ring Sophia's mom gave her when she turned sixteen. Her most cherished possession. She gave it to me three weeks ago when she came through town. To see her ring, she said, she'd have to see me, making me a fact of her life. It was as close to a commitment as she'd ever get.

I took off Sophia's ring and put it on my left hand and slid my ketchup-sticky wedding band onto my right and snorted at my own small gesture. Gemma and I looked at each other in silence a long time. Our server came over and cleared her throat, not wanting to interrupt. She had our bill. Gemma reached for her wallet, no doubt to pull out a card, but Snug only takes cash. I pulled a wad of bills out of my pants pocket and another from an inside jacket pocket; I'd come prepared. I told Gemma it was the least I could do since she'd listened to me all afternoon and evening. I handed the server the cash, including a generous tip, and straightened the remaining bills, refolding them and putting them back in my pocket. Without looking at Gemma, I finished my tale.

"Sophia comes into town at least once a month, more when she can. I'm always first on her '*to do*' list," I half-smiled. "I visit her when I can get away, every few weeks. Sometimes near a movie set. Sometimes a resort or a large city where we can get lost." I sighed, "But, it's only a few days, a short-term diversion."

The front door opened and a lone woman paused in the doorway and looked around. The newcomer was confident and sophisticated and pretty. She smiled and strode to our table. I introduced Gemma, and the newcomer asked if I had plans this coming weekend. I did. With Sophia. She pouted, ran a finger along my cheek, and walked away. I watched her.

Gemma stared, waiting for the explanation.

I shrugged, "I see her when Sophia's out of town."

"*What?*" Gemma gripped the edge of the table. "You're cheating on the woman you've been raving about for hours?"

I stared past her, "Sophia doesn't mind that I see someone else when she's not around." I cleared my throat and swallowed hard, "But, I mind that she does." I whispered, "Some of her is better than none."

I looked down at my hands, splayed on the table. "I have her ring. And that's something."

Gemma covered my hand with hers. "Oh, Simone."

We sat silently again, until I picked up my briefcase from the chair next to me, and Gemma gathered her purse. We stood at the same time. She put her arm through mine and insisted on paying for the cab.

ABOUT THE AUTHORS

LEIGH ALDER

Leigh is a retired English teacher and now a full-time writer. She holds a Master of Professional Writing degree from Towson University. She lives near the university and cares for an emotionally needy cat.

STELLA ALMAZAN

When she's not wielding her stethoscope and reflex hammer, Dr. Stella Almazan writes steamy romance about doctors in love and lust. Always in lipstick and Louboutins. Even in the shower. Stella has forthcoming words in a Running Wild Press anthology. She is delighted to make her debut with Red Penguin Books. @Stella-A_Romance

SKYE BALLANTYNE

Skye Ballantyne has always had the desire to write from a young age. She had stories that she just had to get down onto paper; stories that refused to be silent. They needed to be shared with the world. As she grew, she desired to write a story that would make people feel the same way she did when she read some of her favorite books. She took to writing and hasn't looked back since.

Skye also enjoys helping people and bringing awareness to

different social causes to help make this world a better place to live in, one with more love and acceptance.

Skye has a blog where she writes on a writing prompt each day. Check it out at:

https://scatteredthinker.weebly.com/blog

NATALIE CARROLL

Natalie was first published at the age of 14 and since then has gone onto be published in multiple anthologies. Her aspirations are to be as great as Jk Rowling, John Green, Arthur Doyle and many more of the literature greats!

SHARI HELD

Shari Held is an Indianapolis-based, award-winning fiction author who spins tales of romance, horror, and mystery. Her short stories have been published in numerous magazines and anthologies, including Hoosier Noir, Homicide for the Holidays, Asinine Assassins, and Murder 20/20, for which she served as co-editor. Her short stories have appeared in several Red Penguin Collection anthologies, including Between the Covers and Pets on the Prowl. When not writing, she cares for feral cats and other wildlife, reads, and strategizes imaginative ways for characters and trouble to collide!

DAVID LANGE

David Lange was born and grew up on Long Island, New York. A graduate of the United States Air Force Academy, he served for 30 years as an Active Duty officer in the United States Air Force before retiring in 2018. Colonel Lange is a decorated combat veteran and flew numerous combat, combat support, and humanitarian relief missions during his career. He was awarded the prestigious Institute of Navigation Superior Achievement Award in recognition of his life-long accomplishments as a practicing navigator. David loves sharing stories of hope and inspiration. He has numerous short stories, essays, and poems published within various anthologies and his memoir, "Quest: My Journey Through La Mancha," was published in 2020.

MATT J. MCGEE

MATT McGEE writes short fiction in the Los Angeles area and his story 'Sins of the Father' appeared in Red Penguin Press's recent 'Trick or Treat' issue. "I actually received this voicemail one day, and broken-hearted over the loss of my father and my dog (my life was a country song for a while), I drove across town with my landlady's pool supplies to clean a total stranger's pool." When not typing, Matt drives around in rented cars and plays goalie in local hockey leagues.

ARIK MITRA

Arik Mitra lives in Kolkata, India. An IT professional, he has been writing for three years now. He writes mainly short stories and poetry in english and bengali (mother tongue). His work has been published by Clarendon House Publications, Red Penguin Books, Rosey Ravelston Books-Dyst Journal, Writers and Reader's Magazine and more.

Facebook - https://www.facebook.com/arik.mitra.927
Instagram - https://www.instagram.com/neuralnomad/

TIM O'NEAL

Tim is a part-time time-traveler, romantic, and renaissance man. He's worked in different fields including: wildland firefighting, house construction, sheep farming, and leading spin classes. His myriad of short stories have appeared in YA, romance, and horror publications across the US, UK, and Canada. He lives in the mountains of Colorado and spends his non-writing time exploring the backcountry.

JOSH POOLE AND TRAVIS WELLMAN

Josh Poole is a visual artist and writer working out of a sleep Virginia town. Travis Wellman is a writer living in a remote Washington town who plays with fossils for a living.

LUISA KAY REYES

Luisa Kay Reyes has had pieces featured in "The Raven Chronicles", "The Windmill", "The Foliate Oak", "The Eastern Iowa Review", and other literary magazines. Her essay, "Thank You", is the winner of the April 2017 memoir contest of "The Dead Mule School Of Southern Literature". And her Christmas poem was a first place winner in the 16th Annual Stark County District Library Poetry Contest. Additionally, her essay "My Border Crossing" received a Pushcart Prize nomination from the Port Yonder Press. And two of her essays have been nominated for the "Best of the Net" anthology. With one of her essays recently being featured on "The Dirty Spoon" radio hour.

FLASH FICTION ROMANCE
BONUS MATERIAL

WAITING ROOM

- Anita Haas

He scrawls on a napkin;
She will live.
They told him to keep his cell handy. Just in case.
We'll cook dinner together again; test new recipes, add more spice.
She'll scold and romp with our cats again.
And they asked him to wait ...
We'll revisit Venice, toast glasses of vodka in St. Petersburg, sake in Tokyo.
Tears blur his vision. They fall and smudge the letters;
We'll listen to flamenco and jazz, watch Bogart movies.
... to wait here, outside the Emergency Room.
Just like before.
His heart skips as a nurse approaches.
"Sir..."

———

VERITABLE VALENTINE

- J R Turek

He will never know the soaring heights of my affection, the well of wishes I cradle in my heart, the choir of prayers I say for him each day. He can't know how my heart flutters like a spring breeze through tender garden shoots when he smiles and doesn't know I'm watching. He'll never know the midnight hours I am watchful of his rhythmic breaths, wakeful with worry something wretched will befall us, prayerful we remain untouched by evil. He can never know because I could spend my lifetime searching but never find the words to replace I love you.

———

POST-MODERN LOVE

- Steven Michaels

Greg and Amy hadn't had a moment together for weeks. Given their schedules, they had nearly given up on any spontaneity in their encounters. However, Amy thought she had perfected a seductive glance out of the corner of her right eye, which Greg had yet to notice as he was constantly looking downward at his laptop. Meanwhile Greg had thought he had managed to create a new mating call with the subtle clearing of his throat, which Amy had yet to hear as she was always listening to her audiobook.

Thus is the dance of post-modern love.

ABOUT THE FLASH FICTION AUTHORS

ANITA HAAS

Anita Haas is a differently-abled Canadian writer and teacher based in Madrid, Spain. She has published books on film and flamenco (with her husband, Carlos Aguilar), two novelettes, a short story collection, and articles, poems and fiction in both English and Spanish.

Her most recent work is the bilingual picture book, Chato, the Puppy-Cat/Chato, el Perri-Gato, which she has written, translated, and illustrated, and the sales of which are being donated to local animal shelters.

J R TUREK

J R (Judy) Turek, Superintendent of Poetry for the LI Fair, 2020 Hometown Hero by the East Meadow Herald, 2019 WWBA LI Poet of the Year, NYS 2017 Woman of Distinction, Bards Laureate 2013-2015, 25 years as Moderator of the Farmingdale Creative Writing Group; two Pushcart nominations, editor, workshop leader, and author of six poetry books, the most recent 24 in 24. 'The Purple Poet' lives on Long Island with her soul-mate husband, Paul, her dogs, and her extraordinarily extensive shoe collection. msjevus@optonline.net

STEVEN MICHAELS

Steven Michaels is the pen name of the enthusiast Steve Piscitello who understands you have no idea how to pronounce his actual name. He is the author of Sweet Life of Mystery as well as the co-founder and president of Quabbin Quills, a New England nonprofit for writers looking to be published annually in themed anthologies and whose proceeds benefit publication and scholarship funds. Check out quabbinquills.org for all the info!

9 781637 775233